Midnight Tradition

by

NICOLE PYLAND

Midnight Tradition

Celebrities Series Book #3

Maddox Delaney wasn't all that famous; she was well-known by association. Surrounded by her famous, coupled-off friends, Maddox had thought she had her chance at love. And when that didn't work out, she wondered if she'd ever get another try. A New Year's Eve Party hosted by some of her closest friends isn't really her idea of fun, but it might just be what she needs to mend her broken heart.

Avery Simpson wasn't quite sure how she had ended up at this party. She would much rather be working on her app instead of hanging out by herself at a New Year's Eve party hosted by none other than Peyton Gloss and Dani Wilder. When she's ended up tagging along with her eccentric brother anyway, Avery feels out of place, and she's definitely not planning on kissing anyone at midnight. That is until she meets Maddox.

As the party unfolds, Maddox and Avery not only keep running into each other, they are finding excuses to. What happens when the clock strikes midnight?

One night. One party. One midnight tradition. This is the story of how two women meet and decide to take a chance on something they'd never thought they'd have.

To contact the author or for any additional information visit: **https://nicolepyland.com**

BY THE AUTHOR

Stand-alone books:

- The Fire
- The Moments
- The Disappeared
- Reality Check

Chicago Series:

- Introduction – Fresh Start
- Book #1 – The Best Lines
- Book #2 – Just Tell Her
- Book #3 – Love Walked into The Lantern
- Series Finale – What Happened After

San Francisco Series:

- Book #1 – Checking the Right Box
- Book #2 – Macon's Heart
- Book #3 – This Above All
- Series Finale – What Happened After

Tahoe Series:

- Book #1 – Keep Tahoe Blue

- Book #2 – Time of Day
- Book #3 – The Perfect View
- Book #4 – Begin Again
- Series Finale – What Happened After

Celebrities Series:

- Book #1 – No After You
- Book #2 – All the Love Songs
- Book #3 – Midnight Tradition
- Book #4 – Path Forward
- Series Finale – What Happened After

Sports Series:

- Book #1 – Always More
- Book #2 – A Shot at Gold
- Book #3 – The Unexpected Dream
- Book #4 – Finding a Keeper

CONTENTS

CHAPTER 1

MADDOX needed to get laid. No, that wasn't right. Maddox Delaney needed a girlfriend. She needed a girlfriend she could have sex with, make love with, kiss at midnight, hold hands with, look at the stars at night with, and fall in love with. She'd settle for getting laid, though. It had been a long time.

It had probably been since Kenzie and Lennox's wedding reception. That night had been a good one. A friend of a friend had brought a woman who was single with the intention of setting her up with Maddox. Maddox had been interested. The woman had been, too. They'd had a heated make-out session behind one of the pillars in the reception hall, and when the woman had offered her place up for the rest of their night, Maddox had gone with her. They'd had their night of fun, but it hadn't gone anywhere beyond that.

It was probably a good thing. Maddox hadn't been ready for anything serious at the time. Back then, her long-term relationship had just ended for the second time. She had a rule: fool her once; that kind of a thing. Jessica had already torn her heart out twice, and she wouldn't allow it to happen for the third time. They hadn't spoken to each other since their second breakup. It had been about a year ago when Jessica messaged, asking if they could meet. Maddox had said no, and that had been the end. She had decided, in that moment, that the mysterious pull of her ex-girlfriend would only lead her to heartbreak and misery.

What the hell was she thinking, going to this thing

tonight? She had just returned from a photo shoot in Morocco, and she only had a few hours of sleep and was still dealing with jetlag. Before Morocco, there had been Madrid, and before Madrid, she had been in Paris. It was a lot, but a photographer had to travel. She preferred landscapes and nature shots when she could get the time, but she made her money in fashion these days, which only made having a famous supermodel ex-girlfriend all that more interesting. She'd managed to not run into Jessica at any of her shoots, but that had taken a lot of effort on her part. She wanted to stop thinking about the possibility of running into her. She needed someone new in her life now; someone who would give her those amazing butterflies and make her feel understood and wanted.

"Mad, you have to come," Peyton told her.

"Why?"

"It's my party," Peyton offered as if that should be the only reason needed.

"I just got home, Peyton," Maddox argued as she lay in her bed. "I won't be any fun tonight. It's all about staying up, and I can barely keep my eyes open."

"You'll be fine. You've been traveling forever. You're used to it."

"Peyton, I–"

"It's the first big party since Sienna was born."

"I know."

"She's staying with my parents for the weekend. Dani and I love our daughter, but we could use a little adult time, too. We didn't even do our big summer thing this year. I don't want it to be the end of an era just because she and I started our family or because now that Kenzie and Lennox are married, I somehow see even less of them."

"That's probably more due to Kenzie's big movie deal and Lennox's new gig than their wedding," she returned.

"Maybe, but it's been a while since I've seen my friends. And you're one of my friends, Mad. Come on. It'll be just like old times."

"Except that everyone I know has a husband or a wife, is engaged, or in a serious relationship."

"You wouldn't be the only single person there."

"I don't know, Pey. I was kind of planning on sitting this one out and just going to bed early," she replied.

Maddox moved the phone from one ear to the other.

"If that's what you really want, I won't try to guilt you. I think you'll regret it later, though. It's going to be fun. We're in LA this year. So, no cold weather. Plus, I'm not working or performing or presenting or doing anything that would require me to not be with you guys like I normally am. This time next year, I'll probably have an album out and be ready to go on tour or something."

"So, this is you trying not to guilt me?"

"I'm a good friend. What can I say?" Peyton teased. "Festivities begin at five, remember?"

"Who starts a party at five?"

"Someone that wants to watch the final sunset of the year with her friends and family. You should be there with us, Mad. Let's ring in the new year together."

Maddox disconnected the call after saying goodbye to one of her oldest friends. Peyton was right. Maddox would regret missing this party. She had always been a joiner. When Maddox was on a shoot or at a Fashion Week, she went to the after-parties. That was how she had originally met Jessica. She'd have a few drinks there, talk to some industry people, and maybe even take some photos. They were fun. People usually ended up complimenting her work while there, and sometimes, Maddox got jobs just by being present at an event. Tonight, she wasn't hoping for more work. She could actually use a break from all the time zones. She did miss her friends, though. She missed the old parties Peyton used to throw before they all got older and settled down.

She recalled the summer camp week where Kenzie and Lennox had met. She had been so tired then; she had only half participated in everything. She seemed to recall herself even faking an ankle injury to avoid participating. She had been doing the long-distance thing with Jessica back then. They both traveled for work so much; it was only every so often that they'd be in the same city. The following year's event was actually Peyton and Dani's wedding. That was fun, but Maddox had been their photographer, so it was also work. There had been a few events after that, but not many. It made Maddox sad. Her friends were all moving on, settling down, and having family events now; and she wanted that, too.

"But, first…" Maddox tossed her phone aside and reached between her legs. "Where was I?" she asked herself out loud as she moved under her boy shorts and into her folds.

She'd been ready for an orgasm the entire flight home. During the flight, Maddox had watched a movie on her iPad that wasn't exactly lesbian porn, but it also wasn't something she would want the small child sitting next to her to see, so she had kept it at an angle for the entire two-hour run time. Maddox had been too exhausted when she had first arrived home to do anything, despite how turned on she had been. This morning, though, her body was more than ready, and Maddox knew she needed to come to finally release all the tension she was carrying. That was especially true if she was going to have to go to this party and watch a bunch of happy and in love people kiss each other at midnight.

Maddox used her free hand to open the top drawer of her table and pulled out her small, black vibrator. She hadn't brought it with her, and that had been a mistake. She turned it on and slid it down to where her fingers were slowly stroking her clit. Then, she let it take over and do the work. Her hips rolled a little, and her eyes closed. She pictured no woman in particular, working between her legs. The woman had dark hair, but other than that, she was a faceless entity. Maddox considered that to be a good sign because she used to picture Jessica's face between her legs. This was progress. Her head rolled back a little as she slid the length of the vibrator up and down and then held it in place on a particularly good spot.

When she came, she didn't think about Jessica. She thought about how good the orgasm felt, how much she really wanted another one, and how she wished it had come from someone else. Maddox turned off the vibrator but rubbed it against her clit until she came down all the way. After she caught her breath, she removed it and dropped the useful device somewhere on the bed. Then, she slid her fingers back down and moved them first to her entrance, where she pushed them inside. Her dildo was in a drawer that, due to her position, was too far away for her to reach, and she needed to come again right now. She moved her fingers in and out, not really reaching deep enough for that amazing g-spot orgasm she craved, but curling and thrusting enough to get herself nearly there before she used her other hand to bring her clit back to the edge. The second orgasm that tore through her was even better than the first. It was then, and only then, that she felt like she could actually make it through this party tonight.

It was just after eleven in the morning. Maddox had enough time to take a long, hot bath to help her muscles recover from both the flight and her orgasms. She would eat lunch and take a look at some of the photos she had taken in Morocco to see if any of them had gallery potential. She had been meaning to put another show together, but being so busy with the magazine photo shoots, she hadn't had the time. She decided she would pick out something to wear to head over to Peyton and Dani's place about thirty minutes away and stick around just long enough to be able to share stories and jokes about it later. Then, she would return home, fall into bed, and finally, get some much-needed sleep.

CHAPTER 2

"ANTHONY, I do not want to go to this thing. Come on," Avery said.

"Gross. Don't call me by my Christian name. You know I go by Tony. And why not? It's a Peyton Gloss party. It's going to be amazing."

"Because I don't know Peyton Gloss or any of her famous friends."

"But I do, and you will when you come tonight," Tony argued as Avery stared across the café table at her older brother and gave him a glare. "Peyton really is great, Avery. She may be richer than God, but she's actually really down to earth."

"So, because she's down to earth, I'm supposed to go to her party?"

Tony put both hands on the table and said, "Okay. Look. There's this guy…"

"I knew it! Who is he?" Avery took a drink of her iced mocha.

"His name is Dario. He's Italian."

"Of course, he is," she said.

"He's two years younger than me. He's got a sexy accent, and abs that go with it."

"Dancer?"

"Yes."

"And he's into you?"

"I don't know. I did the makeup on tour, and he hung out with the dancers mostly."

Tony had just returned from another tour where he was the makeup artist. He usually spent the tours flirting and having sex with as many men as humanly possible.

Sometimes, Avery thanked God that her parents had two other kids. Tony was the oldest, she came next, and then Maria and William. Thankfully, Maria and William were both straight. Maria had married her husband a couple of years after she got out of college. They now had a little girl. William had a fiancée and a plan to have the white picket fence in the burbs with her one day. At twenty-seven and twenty-five, respectively, they might just be the only hope for the Simpson clan to continue on for the next generation.

Tony wasn't interested in settling down anytime soon, and even if he did, he had been very clear with their parents that he did not want kids. Tony had come out back in high school, at seventeen, but pretty much everyone had known he was gay well before that. Avery had been sixteen at the time and had been questioning herself. She had first thought about coming out in high school, but after Tony had given his news, she'd wanted to wait until she knew for sure she was gay. After a few years of trying to entertain the idea of being anything other than a lesbian, she finally told her parents. They had been more than surprised, but they were supportive.

"So, I'm really just going to this thing to be your wingwoman," she said.

"But you're the *best* wingwoman," he replied with a fake smile.

"When are you planning on being my wingman?" she tossed back.

"I don't hang out with lesbians," he replied, taking a drink of his iced coffee.

"I'm a lesbian," Avery said with a chuckle.

"You're my sister."

"What about Peyton Gloss? She's married to a woman."

"They've never come out as official lesbians," he argued.

"You're insane." Avery laughed.

Tony then leaned over the table and said, "You bring

me a woman you're interested in, little sister, and I will talk you up like it's nobody's business. I'll tell her how much you love going down on women and that you only care about them in the bedroom."

"Tony!" She laughed louder.

"What? Is it not true? Are you not a giver?"

"I am not talking to my *brother* about sex," she said.

"Honey, if you can't talk to me about it, who can you talk to?"

She thought about that. Tony was her brother. He was a little annoying and a whole lot of extra. That was how he described himself, at least. He was also probably her best friend. Avery had friends, but they were mainly people she worked with. She was also so busy at work that she didn't have time left over to find new friends, and finding friends as an adult wasn't easy. Tony was gone a lot, though. He did at least two tours a year and sometimes more if they were short. He worked music video shoots and a couple of movie shoots when he was between tours, but he loved touring the best. That meant he was gone the majority of the time, and they were reduced to texting or FaceTime to communicate, often with different time zones to compete with.

"Fine. I'll go," she said. "But only until the two of you decide to find some room to hook up in. Maybe have the decency to take him back to your place or go to his place. Don't mount the guy in Peyton Gloss's guest bedroom. I don't think Mom and Dad could take that shame." Avery winked at him.

"Why not? They've handled all the rest of the shame I've brought them pretty well."

"True, but everyone has a limit. Don't test them, Tony."

"Fine. If he is interested, we'll go somewhere else. You should stay until midnight, though. I'm sure she'll have fireworks or something."

"Can she even do that? Are they legal here?" Avery asked, finishing her drink.

"She's Peyton Gloss. I'm sure she paid someone to let her do it."

After hugging her brother goodbye at the café, Avery made her way to her car, which she had parked on the street in the very trendy West Hollywood. Before she climbed in, she noticed a store she hadn't paid any attention to before. It wasn't exactly a store she would see on Rodeo Drive, but it wasn't a thrift shop, either. There were two very nice-looking dresses in the window display. For a second, Avery considered going home and rifling through her closet for something to wear tonight. Then, she clicked the button of her key fob, locking the door back again, and headed inside.

By the time Avery got home, it was three in the afternoon. This party started at five for some reason. She had just enough time to hop in the shower and get dressed before she had to leave. She had offered to drive Tony as well, but he had wanted to drive himself in case he needed to make a quick exit later. Avery slid the dress she had bought – spending way too much money on it – over her body and glanced at herself in the mirror. She normally felt pretty uncomfortable in dresses, preferring a much more casual approach to clothing. Tonight, for some reason she'd yet to uncover, though, she wanted to dress up.

Maybe it was the idea of going to a party at a famous person's house. Well, they were technically two famous people. Avery actually remembered where she was the moment Dani and Peyton had come out, revealing they were not only in a relationship but were engaged to be married. It had been such a big deal, no one could have escaped it if they wanted to. Avery had been in her sister's garage, where she had been working at the time. It had been a makeshift office for her fledgling business. That day, she had been having a hard time with a component and needed a break from work. When she had gone to a random gossip blog, she saw the news. Peyton and Dani had done an interview. Avery had watched the whole thing and couldn't focus on work for the rest of the day. She had smiled pretty much non-stop because she had called it. She had thought they were a couple the entire time, and she had been right. She also smiled because she liked Peyton's music. She knew how influential she was. Having her out and proud in any capacity was a win for Avery and people like her. Having Dani out and proud, too, was a big bonus.

She put on some mascara and a little lipstick but kept the rest of her face clean. Then, she found a pair of short heels in her closet and took another look at herself in the mirror. Her long, dark hair was straight and down to her breasts on either side of her face. She used to wish her hair had more volume, but she'd gotten exactly one perm in her life to try to compensate for that, and that had been a mistake. Ever since then, Avery had been more than okay with her flat hair. She did wonder if she should do something else with it tonight, though. There would be celebrities there. It wouldn't just be Dani and Peyton. Lennox and Kenzie would probably be there, too. They had only just gotten married, and all the magazines and sites talked about how the four women were very close. More famous people would probably be there, too. Many of them would likely be supermodels or actresses. She should do something more to fit in with those beautiful women, right?

She didn't want to stick out like a sore thumb. She looked around her small bedroom. She didn't have a scarf. Did famous people wear scarves? It seemed like something they would wear. Avery knew they liked leggings, too, but that wouldn't be appropriate for the occasion. *Jewelry*, she thought to herself, and rushed, tripping over her heels a little, toward her jewelry box. She wasn't a woman that had fancy jewelry, but she did have a grandmother who had left her a necklace with a single, perfect pearl in the middle. She put it on and returned to her mirror, smiling as she was now satisfied with her look. Then, she glanced at her watch and noticed the time.

"Wish me luck," she said to her own reflection.

CHAPTER 3

MADDOX arrived a little later than she had planned. Initially, she had hoped to get there a little before five and help her friends set up or take some pictures of their beach view without random people to get in her way. Unfortunately, she had hit some traffic on the way and arrived at five-fifteen instead. Noticing a few cars in the long driveway and along the street, she knew she was too late for the unobstructed view of the water and the rocky cliffs to the left. She'd have to catch them next time.

"Mad's here," Peyton yelled when she opened the front door. "And she brought booze? Maddox, why would you bring booze? You know we have everything."

"It's a hostess gift. It's wine, Peyton." She passed Peyton the bottle of red that she had brought. "And I got it at the grocery store, so I'm pretty sure it's terrible."

"It's fine. Dani's the person who likes good wine. I don't really care."

"Then, don't let her drink it," Maddox replied.

Peyton winked at her and gave her a conspiratorial expression before Dani made her way into the foyer.

"Hey, Mad. Come on in. Len and Kenz are out on the beach already."

"Cool. Are they the only ones here? I saw a bunch of cars. Did you invite the entire city to this thing?"

"The staff she hired is setting up," Dani explained. "And there are a couple more people here. I'll introduce you on your way outside."

Maddox followed Dani and Peyton into the house. Peyton went toward the kitchen to drop off the wine and probably to check on the caterers. Dani introduced Maddox to the few people who had already arrived. One of them was a model Dani knew. There was one of Peyton's producers with his wife, and then there were Peyton's younger sisters. Well, two of the three. One of them was out of town and couldn't make the party. Dani opened the glass door that led to their massive deck, swimming pool, and jacuzzi. Maddox never really noticed those things, though. She only saw the strip of yellow sand and the beauty that was the Pacific Ocean beyond it. There were a few people walking around on the private beach, but other than that, it was pretty calm outside of the party things Peyton had obviously placed in all the right spots for the event tonight. Maddox turned her camera, which she always brought with her, toward the cliffs to get a few shots in. It wasn't her best or even the most expensive camera. It was a more compact model that made it easier to throw in a backpack or purse and hit the road. It did the trick, though, and she could always edit if she needed to later.

"Hey, thanks for coming," Peyton said as she joined her. Maddox immediately turned her camera toward the beauty and took several quick shots. "Mad, we've talked about this," she scolded.

"I know, but you're standing right there in my way. What was I supposed to do?" she teased.

"Taking pictures of my wife?" Dani asked as she approached and wrapped her arms around Peyton from behind.

"Yup." Maddox snapped a few of the two of them together. "You two are just so damn photogenic."

"Are those going online?" Dani asked, kissing Peyton's neck sweetly.

"No. I'll send them to you guys, though," Maddox offered. "I'm not working tonight, I promise."

"The sun's about to set," Peyton said. "You should be

taking pictures of that, Maddox Delaney." She pointed out to the sky.

"I was until you two interrupted me." She chuckled and turned back to the water. "It is beautiful, isn't it?"

"I love that we live here," Dani said.

"Me too," Peyton added. "Mad, how's the hunt for a new place going for you?"

"Terrible. I'm so tired of renting. I want to buy a place and really make it mine, but I'm either working too much and can't get to a place I like online until it's already gone, or I go, and I don't like it when I see it."

"Do you want our realtor's name? Maybe you just need a new person on the job," Peyton offered.

"I don't think the kind of houses you're buying would be the same kind of house I'm thinking about buying. That realtor would be taking a major hit to their commission if they took me on. I'm looking for a two-bedroom non-beachfront property *without* a movie theater and game room inside."

"Says the woman who spends a lot of time in both of those places when she visits this place," Dani said.

"Your sarcasm is rubbing off on her," Maddox said to Peyton. "I'm not sure I like it."

"It's been years; time to get used to it, Mad," Peyton returned, patting Maddox's shoulder more sarcastically than sympathetically.

"Where are Lennox and Kenzie? I thought you said they were here." Maddox asked.

"They're probably making out around that corner." Peyton pointed to a gap between her house and some rocks. "There's this little space in there *I know* they go to sometimes to be alone whenever they're here. You've been warned; one or both of them might be naked."

"They wouldn't." Maddox's eyes went wide.

"They have," Dani said as if it was the most normal thing in the world. "Don't tell Kenzie we know this. Lennox won't care, but Kenzie might. Our room overlooks the water and those rocks. We saw a certain person with a hand inside bikini bottoms once while the other person was pressed against the rocks."

"Please tell me you looked away," Maddox said.

"She called me over," Peyton replied with a wide smile. "Then, we looked away."

"You guys are terrible," Maddox said as she laughed. "I'm going to avoid the rocks and take some pictures facing that way." She pointed at the cliffs.

"Okay. I have passed appetizers happening in about ten minutes, and the bar's open already. I'm going to see if anyone else has arrived." She kissed Dani on the cheek.

"Always the hostess, my wife."

And that, she was. Peyton Gloss had been hosting parties like this for what felt like decades now. Maddox had known Dani before Peyton, though. She had had a friend post some of her work online, Dani had seen it, and they had met up after that. All of a sudden, Maddox's work was everywhere. She had offers coming in left and right. Only some of them were what she really wanted to do. Other offers were fashion-related. She liked fashion, and it paid the bills, but over the past few years, Dani had gotten into photography more than modeling. She and Maddox would go out on day hikes sometimes and take pictures of the scenery and the animals. Maddox would teach her different settings and how to get just the right shot of a bird in flight. It had brought Maddox even closer to this group of celebrity women. They were her very best friends in the world – more like her family, and she loved them dearly.

Maddox kicked off her shoes right before her feet hit the sand, and she adjusted to its give as her feet pressed into it deeply. There was just something about the feel of sand between her toes. She hadn't dressed up for the party, knowing Peyton wouldn't expect her to be in formal wear. She had put on a pair of black Capri pants specifically because she wanted to walk along the beach and maybe even wade out a little into the water. Her light-blue button-down shirt matched her eyes, or at least that was what she'd been told the few times she had worn it.

She wasn't sure how long she'd been gone, but by the time she turned back toward the house, the sun was gone, and the only lights were coming from the few houses that lined the beach. She had taken several good shots – or at least, she hoped they were good. She would have to check them out at home on her big monitor later. She could now hear the sounds of the party as she approached from the beach. She picked up her shoes first, headed to the water to rinse as much of the sand from her feet as possible, then slid her shoes back on and headed toward the patio. From this far away, she could make out a few people she knew and some she didn't. No one was in the pool or the hot tub, despite both being available thanks to the particularly hot, even for Los Angeles, day and now, evening.

Her eyes came upon a woman she didn't know. She was wearing a very nice, flowy-looking dress that Maddox couldn't make out the color of in the dim lighting. She also had a white sweater over it. The woman's hair was long and dark, and it framed her face nicely, despite the ocean wind trying to blow it away slightly. Maddox couldn't tell the color of her eyes from where she was standing, but she *could* tell they were thoughtful. They were soulful. Maddox had gotten good, thanks to her years of photography experience, at seeing things in the eyes of her subjects. She picked up her camera, adjusted a few settings, and took a couple of pictures. The sound from the camera caused the woman to look Maddox's way. She didn't smile or frown, though; her expression was just unreadable. Maddox was about to say something. Well, she would have to kind of yell it from how far away she was, but before she could, a man approached the woman's right, and the woman's attention shifted to him. Maddox lowered the camera and made her way up the side steps of the patio and into the house.

"Hey, Maddox," Lennox Owen greeted her.

"Hey, Len," Maddox replied and gave Lennox a one-armed hug. "Let me just put this thing down. I'll come right back." She held up the camera.

"She did hire a photographer tonight specifically with you in mind," Lennox said of Peyton.

"What? Why?"

"Because she wants you to socialize without a camera between you and the people you're socializing with," Lennox stated. "You should really listen to her. I mean, she tried the same thing with Kenz, and look how that worked out."

"You're only saying that because you two just had sex over by some rocks," Maddox teased.

"We did not." Lennox laughed. "Kenzie is amazing, but parties aren't the easiest thing in the world for her. We went out there so she could just have a moment."

"So, you've never had sex out there?"

"No, we have." Lennox winked at her. "But not tonight."

"Where is your wife?"

"Ah, I am still getting used to hearing that." Lennox's perfect smile widened.

"Sounds good, doesn't it?"

"I don't know what it is, but… Yes. I'm lucky just to have her, but there's something about being her wife that just always sounds so perfect to me."

"I'll be right back," Maddox said without waiting for Lennox's response to Kenzie's whereabouts.

She wanted a wife of her own one day. She'd used to think she had found a possibility in Jessica. The first time they'd broken up had been right after that Fourth of July party, where she had met Kenzie Smyth for the first time. It was the same week-long event where Lennox met her future wife and where Peyton proposed to Dani. Maddox had been so happy back then. She had even given Kenzie a pep talk, using her relationship with Jessica as an example. Little did she know; Jessica was sleeping with one of the designers she was working with at the time.

The affair hadn't gone on long, according to her ex-girlfriend, and it had been mainly due to the distance between her and Maddox. Maddox had found out about this affair during their three-week vacation after the camp with her friends, and she had ended things between them then. At the time, she could see nothing beyond the pain of that betrayal.

A few months later, though, Jessica had asked for another chance, and Maddox had given in. She had loved her. She had also felt guilty about the distance and started taking more jobs where they could be together. Things were going well for a while, and Maddox had considered proposing. She had even looked at rings. Then, the fighting had started. During one of those fights, Jessica had admitted to kissing another woman. She'd apologized, begged, and asked for forgiveness. She had also promised it would never happen again and tried to say that it meant nothing. They hadn't slept together, after all. But Maddox had left for good then. She knew now she would never go back. That was just who Jessica was, and Maddox didn't want someone that wanted someone else, even if it was just a kiss. She wanted a woman that only wanted her; that only wanted to kiss her for the rest of their lives.

"Oh, sorry," the voice came from the body that bumped into Maddox as she tried to make her way through the kitchen to the expansive living room.

"It's okay," Maddox replied without even seeing the person. Then, she looked over and saw the woman from the patio that she had seen earlier. "Oh, hi."

"Hi. Sorry, I wasn't paying attention," the woman said with a smile that was cautious and held something back.

"It happens at parties. No worries," Maddox said, smiling back at her.

"Hey, Avery?" a male voice said from somewhere else.

The woman looked behind Maddox and said, "Excuse me."

She then walked around Maddox, and Maddox felt the

arm brush up against her own, causing goosebumps to pop up on her skin. Maddox turned her head slightly to catch the woman as she walked away, taking in the scent of lilacs with her.

"Mad, you don't have a drink," Peyton said.

"What?" Maddox turned back to see her friend standing in front of her, holding a champagne flute. "Oh, thanks." She looked beyond Peyton to see Dani talking to Lennox and one of Peyton's sisters. "It doesn't look like your wife has a drink, either, Pey."

Peyton turned her head, smiled, and replied, "She's not in a champagne mood."

"Hey, Peyton?"

"Yeah?" Peyton turned back to her.

"Who's that?" Maddox moved to stand beside Peyton and faced the woman and the man she was speaking with; the same guy from the patio.

"Oh, that's Tony. He's been on my tour crew a few times."

"No, I mean the woman with him," Maddox clarified, taking a long drink from her champagne.

"Oh, I don't know."

"You don't know?"

"No. I didn't even know Tony was here. I invited him, but Dani must have let him in. Everyone got a plus one. I don't know who she is. Why?"

"No reason," Maddox said.

Peyton turned her head toward her in amusement and asked, "No reason?"

Maddox had been caught.

"She just bumped into me earlier, and I didn't know who she was, so I thought I'd ask you since this is your party."

"Really?"

"Peyton, do not do what I think you're going to do; what your face is telling me you're thinking about doing right now," Maddox warned.

18

"What do you think I'm going to do?" Peyton squinted at her.

"You're going to try to introduce us or something," Maddox answered.

"And *why* would I do that?"

"You know why."

"Kenzie and Lennox are married, Mad. I did that," Peyton pointed out.

"I'm pretty sure *they* had something to do with that, Peyton."

"I just meant that I am responsible for them meeting. I knew they had a thing for each other, so I made sure they were both in the same place at the same time."

"Well, *they* had a thing for each other. I don't even know who *she* is," Maddox explained.

"You won't know until you introduce yourself."

"She's with someone, Peyton. She's here on a date."

"With Tony?" Peyton chuckled. "I doubt it."

"Why?"

"Because Tony is beyond gay, and I'm pretty sure the only reason he came tonight was because Dario is here, and he has a thing for him."

"Oh," Maddox replied.

"So, do you want me to say hi to Tony and get introduced to his plus one?" Peyton asked.

"No, it's fine. I really was just curious." Maddox shook her head. "I'm going to see if I can find some people I know now that a few more people are here. I have to kill time somehow, right?"

CHAPTER 4

"HEY, Tony," Peyton Gloss said as she approached them.

"Oh, hey." Tony gave Peyton a quick hug. "Thanks for the invite."

"Please, like you're here to hang out with me. I know you're only here for Dario," she replied and gave him a playful glare.

"He's just so pretty," Tony replied.

"That, he is." Peyton turned to Avery. "Hi, I'm Peyton," she greeted and held out her hand for Avery to shake.

"Oh, sorry. Peyton, this is my sister, Avery. Avery, this is Peyton," Tony finally managed to introduce.

"Sister?" Peyton said with an interesting expression on her face.

"That's me," Avery replied, wondering how lame that comment was in her head the moment she said it out loud.

"Well, it's nice to meet you. And thanks for coming."

"Thank you for letting me tag along. You have a beautiful home," Avery said, trying to recover from the first two words she had said to the biggest superstar in the world.

"Of course." Peyton's smile was wide and genuine. "Do you have a drink?"

"Not yet, no. We've just been walking around."

"Tony, you didn't get your sister a drink?"

"She's my sister, not my date," Tony replied.

"Speaking of," Peyton began. "Dario is over there." She nodded in the direction of the long hallway that led to the formal dining area. "I saw him come in a few minutes ago."

Tony shook both of his hands and said, "I should wait, right? I shouldn't appear desperate."

"What if you don't go to him now, and he finds someone else to kiss at midnight?" Avery asked.

"Shit. You're right. How do I look?"

"Desperate," Peyton and Avery said at the same time.

"I hate both of you." Tony walked off as Peyton and Avery both laughed.

"So, what do you do?" Peyton asked. "Are you in the arts, too?"

"No, I–"

"Hey, babe, can you come over here for a second?" Dani half-yelled to Peyton from the other room.

"Excuse me," Peyton said, placing a kind hand on Avery's forearm and offering her an equally as kind smile.

Avery stood alone in the middle of a giant room of people. Peyton and Dani's house really was magnificent. They knew how to decorate. The place was light and airy, and the furniture was old-school with a modern twist. It looked comfortable and soft instead of blocky and unattractive, like most modern designs that didn't appeal to Avery. She had gotten the brief tour when she and Tony had first arrived. They had free rein of the house. Peyton and Dani had a theater and a game room on the second floor. Most of the bedrooms were on the third. Avery didn't see the need to go up there, but she didn't see a problem with checking out the rooms on the second floor. She also knew there was a balcony that overlooked the water.

Tony had told her that Peyton and Dani had only moved into this place a few months prior. They had bought it well before that but had to remodel and refurbish a lot of it. Then, with Sienna coming along, they'd waited until the dust had literally settled before moving in. According to Tony, the two women were now up to nine properties all over the world. That seemed like a lot of work to Avery, but Tony had explained that they had to do something with all that money. Avery had no idea what that must feel like.

She made her way up the steps, passing a couple holding hands on their way down. She smiled at them, recognizing one of them as an actor on her favorite TV show and the other as the girlfriend she had seen in a couple of movies. Avery looked away after giving them a polite smile, not wanting them to think she was one of *those* fans. At the top of the stairs, she looked at the open, loft-like space where there was basically another living room. A few people were sitting on the sofas, talking. The music that was playing over the in-room speakers was different than the music playing downstairs. It was softer down there and a little louder up here. Plus, it was jazz downstairs. Up here, it seemed, they had changed the music to pop and top forty hits. She nodded at some people she didn't know as they nodded at her. Then, she turned left to walk down the hall toward the open double doors.

The theater had eight reclining seats and a front row with two small sofas. It was much larger than she had imagined. Then again, she hadn't seen many in-house movie theaters in person. Tony socialized with these people. She really didn't. There was nothing playing on the massive screen at the front of the room, and no one was inside. She turned around, made her way back through the living area and toward the game room. The room itself was the size of two bedrooms, or maybe even three smaller ones. It had a pool table and a ping-pong table as well as a bar off to the side and two old-school arcade games already being played by two men she didn't recognize. The pool table had three people around it with cues, talking and laughing. The ping-pong table was empty, but there was a bartender behind the bar and two people in line for a drink. Avery decided to stand in this line, since it was likely shorter than the one downstairs, and get herself a drink. It would help calm her nerves.

"Hey, Maddox."

Avery turned at the sound of a voice she thought she recognized to see Kenzie Smyth standing next to the woman she had bumped into earlier downstairs. They must have just walked into the room behind her.

"Hey, Kenz," the woman replied.

Avery turned back to the bar. She didn't want to appear to be eavesdropping.

"Need a drink?" Kenzie asked her.

"Yeah. You?"

"This line is always shorter," Kenzie said. "I need to grab one for Lennox, too. She's downstairs, talking to another writer about how to better create appropriate tension between two future love interests without giving away that they're going to be love interests later."

"Ah, the life of a writer," the woman, Avery now knew as Maddox, replied as the two women joined her in line.

"What are you up to right now?" Kenzie asked her.

"Just standing in line with you," Maddox replied.

Avery smiled at that.

"I mean, with work."

"Taking a short break. I have to be in Paris again in a few weeks for a shoot, and then, I'm doing something for National Geographic in Ireland after that."

"That's cool," Kenzie said.

"Yes, I love working with them. I get to be outside, taking pictures of the world, not just women in dresses."

"What can I get you?" the bartender asked Avery, and she realized she hadn't been paying attention to the fact that she was now the next in line.

"Oh, can I just get a rum and Coke?" she asked.

"Sure," he replied and began mixing her drink.

"Can you just make that two?" Maddox moved up beside her. "If it's easier to do at the same time." She turned to Avery. "Sorry, I'm not cutting the line. I just heard you order the drink I was going to get for myself."

"No, it's fine." Avery smiled at her.

Maddox smiled back, and it was nice. No, it was more than nice. It was beautiful. Her eyes were smiling, too. They were this light-blue that was even more beautiful because the shirt matched their shade. The bartender placed their drinks on the bar. Avery didn't know if she was supposed to tip the guy or not. Maddox and Kenzie were watching her now. She didn't want them to think she didn't know what to do.

"Peyton always tips them very well. You don't need to worry about it," Maddox told her, taking her drink from the bar. "Trust me, they're well taken care of."

"Thanks," Avery replied gratefully and picked up her own glass.

"I'm Maddox," the woman said, offering her free hand for Avery to shake. "A friend of Peyton and Dani's." Avery shook her warm, soft hand. "Well, I guess that's true for all of us, huh?"

"Not me." Avery let go of Maddox's hand regretfully when the woman pulled it away. "My brother knows Peyton."

"Brother?" Maddox asked.

"Tony Simpson. He's a makeup artist on her tour. I'm just his guest for the night."

"This is Kenzie," Maddox introduced, taking a drink of her rum and Coke.

"Hi," Kenzie said to Avery after she placed her own order with the bartender. "Nice to meet you."

"You too. I've seen all your movies," Avery replied and instantly closed her eyes in embarrassment. "Sorry… You must get that a lot."

Kenzie smiled at her and said, "It's okay." She then looked over at Maddox. "I should go find my wife." She took the two drinks off the bar. "It was nice to meet you."

"You too," Avery replied.

Then, she took a healthy swig of the rum and Coke she had ordered. When she turned back, Maddox was staring at her with those now focused and intense eyes.

"Well, I should let you get back to your brother." The woman turned to go.

"He's with this guy he's interested in," Avery said

quickly, and Maddox stopped at that and looked over at her. "I don't know why he brought me, really. He said he needed a wingwoman, but Tony's never needed a wingman or woman in his life. He's the consummate extravert, unlike me."

Maddox gave her a small smile and asked, "It's only six. There are still many, many hours to go before the ball drops, so to speak. I asked Peyton if I could display some of the pictures I took earlier on the big screen in the theater room for a few minutes. She said that was fine. Do you want to join me? We can close the door and shut out the party for a bit."

"I don't want to intrude on–"

"You're not," Maddox interjected.

"Okay. That would be nice, I guess." Avery nodded.

She followed Maddox to the theater, where Maddox had already stashed her camera bag. Avery didn't know where to sit, so she just sat in the front row on one of the sofas. Maddox didn't speak as she connected her camera to the system, turned the lights in the room down to just barely on, and closed the doors. Then, she grabbed the remote from the table and sat down next to Avery.

"So, photographer?" Avery asked.

"Yeah, I'm mostly doing fashion right now, but I get to do some nature stuff every now and then."

"Like Ireland?" Avery asked.

Maddox looked over at her, smiled, and asked, "You heard that?"

"Sorry." Avery lowered her gaze to Maddox's hand, which was on the remote. "I didn't mean to eavesdrop."

"It's okay. Yes, is the answer. I'm going to Paris for a fashion thing, but then I get to do an awesome shoot with snakes in Ireland."

"I thought there were no snakes in Ireland. Isn't that the whole reason for St. Patrick's Day?" She took a drink and placed her glass down on a coaster.

Maddox turned on the screen and said, "They have

them in the zoos and stuff. They're bringing some cool species in, though, and I get to photograph them. It should be fun."

"How'd you get into photography?"

It was a terrible question. She had just met this woman. Maddox had only been nice to her because she probably seemed like a lost puppy at a party. This woman surely didn't plan on talking to someone like Avery all night when she had friends like Lennox Owen and Kenzie Smyth – not to mention Peyton Gloss and Dani Wilder – to talk to.

Maddox pressed a few buttons on the remote and replied, "I was always into it. Even when I was a kid, I had a camera. My parents got me this old Polaroid when I was about ten. I was always saving up my allowance to buy film for it because I took pictures of everything."

"What did you do with them?" Avery asked, smiling at the thought of a tiny Maddox walking around with a giant Polaroid camera.

"Hung them with thumbtacks on my bedroom walls. My parents weren't thrilled about that, but they let me get away with it."

"That was nice of them," Avery said.

"Oh, sorry." Maddox wasn't looking at her; she was staring at the screen. "Actually, no, I'm not. That's a good picture of you, given the lighting."

"Huh?" Avery turned to the screen to see herself standing on the patio of this very house. "Oh."

"You looked thoughtful," Maddox said. "Were you thinking about something important?"

"Let's go in here and see if–" The door opened, revealing Lennox and Kenzie, who then entered the room. "Shit. Sorry, Mad."

"It's okay."

"What are you guys doing in here?" Lennox asked, looking back and forth between them.

"Looking at pictures I took earlier. What are you two doing in here?" Maddox asked.

"Kenz and I just wanted a moment alone. Hi, I'm Lennox."

"I know." Avery gave a small wave. "Avery."

"Nice to meet you. This is my wife, Kenzie." Lennox held Kenzie's hand.

"We met, actually," Avery told her.

"When I was getting us drinks," Kenzie added as she leaned into her wife's body.

"I guess we'll leave you two alone," Lennox said.

"You guys can come in," Maddox replied. "We're really just looking at some stuff I took before and after sunset tonight."

For some reason, Avery didn't want Lennox and Kenzie to come in and sit down with them. She had liked the fact that she and Maddox had the room to themselves; that they had started getting to know one another. She didn't know why, but it seemed like it mattered.

CHAPTER 5

WHY had she done that? Maddox loved her friends, but she didn't want them in here with her and Avery. She had only gotten up enough courage to stand next to this woman in line because Kenzie had noticed her staring when they were behind Avery and had given Maddox the nudge to talk to her. Kenzie, of all people, had given her the courage to talk to this woman. She then convinced Avery to join her in the theater because she knew it would be quiet, and they could talk. Now, she'd invited Lennox and Kenzie to join them, which wouldn't give them the privacy she'd wanted to get to know the woman she had caught herself staring at a few times already tonight.

"Can we go to the balcony instead?" Kenzie asked. "There's a bonfire out there now that the sun is down."

"Sure," Lennox said, smiling at her wife. "We'll leave you two to your pictures."

The door closed behind them. Avery looked over at Maddox, who turned back to look at her. Avery's long hair was perfectly straight now that the wind wasn't moving through it. It looked soft. Maddox wanted to touch it. Avery's eyes, now that she could see them up close, were different.

"Your eyes," she said.

"What about–"

"The colors are–"

"Oh, yes. I have one green; one blue. Sorry, I forget sometimes."

"Forget that you have two different-colored eyes?"

"Forget that it's a cool thing to some people."

"It *is* cool," Maddox said with a smile.

"Not to me, but I was born with it. It's called heterochromia. I'm the only one in my family with it. Don't know why."

"Your parents don't—" Maddox continued to stare at her eyes.

"No. My mom has green eyes, and my dad has blue ones. I have three siblings, and none of them have it." Avery shrugged.

"Your eyes are beautiful."

"Really?" Avery asked, turning toward the screen and away from Maddox. She had obviously made the woman uncomfortable, which hadn't been Maddox's intention. "I got made fun of a lot over them as a kid, so I kind of just see it as a nuisance. Try having this thing and filling out any forms that require you to indicate your eye color. You get one option." She held up one long, thin finger with a short, well-kept fingernail.

"I guess I hadn't thought of that," Maddox replied, staring at the finger even as Avery lowered her hand to her lap. "So, the pictures?"

"Yeah… We can move past this one." Avery pointed at the photo of herself on the big screen.

"Why? I like it," Maddox said, smiling at the picture she had taken. "You look thoughtful, like I said."

"I don't remember thinking of anything specific. Maybe just about the water or the sea air or something." Avery chuckled.

Maddox liked the sound of that chuckle. They sat there on the sofa side by side as Maddox flipped through the pictures slowly, one by one. They didn't say a lot. The noise from outside the room kept growing louder and louder. Eventually, Maddox knew she would have to go back out to the party. She didn't want to lose this, though. Avery had leaned over just a little bit toward Maddox. Maddox had scooted over slightly as well. Only a foot of space was between them now. Maddox swallowed as she thought about what to do next. She didn't know this woman at all, but she wanted to spend the rest of the night getting to know her.

"Mad, you're still in here?" Peyton asked after opening the door and breaking the spell.

"We just finished," she said, turning toward her friend.

"Cool. A few people were wondering if they could put the Rocking New Year's Eve on in here since the screen is so big."

"Sure." Maddox stood up reluctantly. "Just let me disconnect the camera stuff."

Maddox moved to where she'd connected the camera earlier, disconnected it, and put everything back into her camera bag. She tucked it away in a far corner so that no one would see it or step on it, and looked up to see that Avery was gone, and five other people had just entered the room. They immediately sat on the recliners and the sofa. Two more entered as Peyton changed the input to the television and put on the show. Another several people then walked in and stood off to the side with their drinks. The music outside the room was much louder now than it had been when she and Avery had first come in here. It felt claustrophobic to her now, so she moved around the people and went out to find Avery. She looked around the space, seeing several people on the sofa and in the chairs, all talking and laughing. Maddox went to the game room, didn't see her there, and decided to make her way to the balcony.

"Hey," she greeted Lennox and Kenzie, who were sitting in two chaise lounges, holding their hands together between them. "Have you seen Avery?"

"No, I thought she was with you," Lennox replied, looking up at her.

"She was, but then a bunch of people came in, and she left."

"She sounds like me," Kenzie said.

Maddox didn't know how to respond to that. Kenzie had Asperger's. She was open about that now, but she didn't always use to be. It had taken meeting Lennox and falling in love with her to help break Kenzie out of her shell. Maddox knew she still struggled at events like this, which was why they spent some time alone together every so often at Peyton's big parties.

"Did she ditch you or something?" Lennox asked.

"I don't know. Maybe." Maddox sat down on one of the two remaining lounges but faced her friends instead of the water. "We were just looking at pictures. Then, Peyton came in and asked for the room. I turned around, and she was gone."

"You guys just met, though, right?" Lennox asked.

"Yes."

"Maybe she had more people to meet, or someone she knew had arrived, and she saw them outside the theater." She shrugged.

"I guess. It *is* a party," Maddox reasoned.

"Is she nice?" Kenzie asked.

"I don't know. I think so. We only talked for, like, an hour."

"And you like her?" Lennox asked.

"I don't know her."

"But you want to get to know her?" Kenzie suggested.

"Maybe." Maddox glanced out at the water, which was now only visible thanks to the bonfire and some torches Peyton had undoubtedly asked someone to set up right near the water's edge.

"Then, find her," Lennox said with a soft laugh. "Mad, it's a New Year's Eve party. Have some fun. You look like you're Peyton's hostage or something." She lightly slapped Maddox's knee with the hand that was not holding Kenzie's.

"I didn't actually want to come tonight."

"What? Why not?" Kenzie asked.

"I'm exhausted. I've gotten a few hours of sleep, at most. You guys know how it is. I've been bouncing from place to place, time zone to time zone, and I haven't caught up on my beauty sleep."

"You're beautiful as is, Maddox. You don't need

beauty sleep," Kenzie said sweetly.

"I'm not jealous because she married me," Lennox replied, teasing her wife.

Kenzie gave Lennox a look for a moment that said she didn't understand. Then, she smiled and nodded. Damn. These two really were perfect for one another.

"I was hoping for a chill night at home. I'd planned on sleeping through the new year. I mean, you've seen one, you've seen them all, right?"

"I don't think that's the case," Lennox replied. "The first one I had with Kenzie was different than any I had experienced before."

"For me too," Kenzie said, staring out over the water. "And this one is, too. It's the first one since we got married."

"Every year is filled with different firsts, Mad."

"You're a wise woman, Lennox Owen," Maddox teased.

"Yeah. So are you. If you want to hang out with us, feel free. We're just watching the fire and the people around it, talking about our year and what's next. If you want to go find someone you might want to spend some time with, I think that's a much better use of your time; but that's just me," Lennox said.

"Am I an asshole because I don't want to hang out with people at my friend's party?" she asked.

"No," Kenzie replied.

"You're not an asshole, Maddox," Lennox added for her wife. "You're tired. We get it. I once spent a single day in four countries on a press junket, and I did the same thing in three countries the next day. Everything is close together in Europe when you're looking at a map. It's much different when you're in the air or on a train bouncing from place to place, though. If you really want to spend the final night of the year in bed alone, just head home. Peyton and Dani will understand. They always do."

Maddox stood up and leaned over the railing, staring

down at the sand and the water beyond it, listening to the sounds of the waves crashing mixed with people talking and laughing. Then, she saw her. Avery was standing off to the side of a small group of people with her arms crossed over her chest. Maddox couldn't make out the expression on her face, but she could tell she was slightly uncomfortable.

"I'll see you guys later, okay?" Maddox turned to her friends.

"Are you going home?" Kenzie checked.

"Not yet."

"We'll be down in a bit. Peyton won't let us hide up here forever," Lennox said.

"See you later, then," Maddox repeated with a smile.

She made her way back downstairs and decided to stop by the bar first to grab them both another rum and Coke. Avery had finished her drink upstairs. Maddox had left her own behind in the theater without having finished it. The line wasn't too long, but it still took a few minutes to get the drinks. She turned and prepared to go outside to, hopefully, still find Avery where she had last seen her, when she was greeted by a familiar face.

"Hey, Maddie," Jessica greeted.

Maddox nearly dropped both glasses. Her grip on them tightened so much, she worried she might crack the glass.

"Jess?"

"Hi," Jessica greeted again with a soft smile.

"What are you doing here?"

"I came with Burke," she replied and nodded to one of the designers she had worked for a few times. "He asked if I wanted to be his plus one. I was in town and didn't have plans, so I said yes. I wasn't sure if you'd be here."

"Well, I am. You should go."

Jessica glanced down at the two glasses in Maddox's hands and said, "You're here with someone?"

"That's really none of your business, Jess."

"But, you are?"

"I'm at a party at my friend's house, Jessica."

"I realize that. Can we just talk, Maddie?" the woman asked.

"What? No."

"Mad, come on. It's been a while now. We can talk about this." Jessica placed an unwanted hand on Maddox's hip.

"Jessica, I don't want to talk to you." Maddox moved back a step to get out of the woman's grasp. "I'm just here to ring in the new year, go home, and get some much-needed sleep."

"Alone?"

"Are you kidding me right now? You have to be. You can't possibly be asking if I'm seeing someone when you–"

"Maddie, I messed up. I made a mistake. But I've been trying to make it up to you."

"Really? So, you tried to make up for sleeping with someone else by kissing *another* someone else to me? How's that going for you?"

"I told you, she kissed me. And yes, I kissed her back, but it was only because you were gone, and I missed you."

"Bullshit, Jess. I don't even think you believe that."

"Mad, you weren't around. Every break you had, you went somewhere else trying to take pictures."

"I went with you to every Fashion Week show, Jessica. I did the best I could with my schedule. We were fighting all the time anyway. It was only a matter of time before you cheated again. Why are we even talking about this? We broke up a long time ago. Don't you have a new girlfriend?"

"We broke up."

"Did you cheat?"

"No." Jessica glared at her. "I didn't cheat on her. She went back to her ex."

"And you're trying to get back together with yours now out of revenge?"

"I'm not trying to do anything other than talk to you, Maddox."

"We talked, Jessica. We talked for days, weeks, and months. We tried twice. I loved you. Hell, I thought I'd marry you one day. And you just treated me like crap. It ended. Again. I never should have taken you back in the first place, but I'm definitely not doing it again."

"I didn't ask you to," Jessica returned, crossing her arms over her chest. "Full of yourself much, Maddox?"

"Then, what could you possibly want to talk about with me?"

"I thought enough time had passed that we could have a civilized conversation. I guess I was wrong." She turned to walk off.

"Jessica, wait." Maddox sighed and took a few steps to catch up to the woman. "I'm sorry. It's just the first time we've seen each other in a long time. I guess I'm not handling it well."

"It's my fault." Jessica sighed as well as she turned back to face her. "I should have told you I was coming tonight. I guess I wanted the element of surprise to see how you'd react."

Jessica's hazel eyes had always been a weakness for Maddox, but it was her smile that typically made Maddox weak in the knees. As Jessica smiled at her now, though, Maddox didn't feel those butterflies in her stomach. She didn't feel the desire that used to bubble over in her every time she saw this woman. She also wished she felt nothing at all around her, but that wasn't the case, either.

"I should go," Maddox said.

"Right. You have a drink to deliver," Jessica replied and pointed to the glasses.

"I do," Maddox stated without giving away that she was here on her own and that this drink was for a woman she had only just met. "Have a good night, Jess."

"You too. Happy New Year."

"Yeah," Maddox said.

She walked around her ex-girlfriend, trying to get rid of the anger and anxiety that Jessica always caused these days. Every memory of their relationship had come flooding back to her the moment she'd laid eyes on Jessica. There had been so many happy moments shared between them. First, they were friends, just getting to know one another. Then, they were sharing an unexpected first kiss. Their hot and fast first time together had been immediately followed by their slow and sexy second time together. And their fourth date, where they'd gone to play paintball, had ended up with them on the ground, rolling around with pastel paint colors dotting their skin and clothing.

The sad moments emerged, too, though. There was their first fight when Maddox had wanted Jessica to meet her family, but Jessica hadn't been ready. They'd fought. Then, they had stopped talking to each other for a few days. Then, they made up in a bar bathroom. There were other fights, of course. Some of them were stupid, but most of them mattered.

The moment Jessica informed Maddox of her affair had been one of the worst in Maddox's life. Somehow, though, the fact that, even after that – even after Maddox had forgiven her and had taken her back – Jessica had still kissed someone else, bothered Maddox more than the fact that Jessica had been sleeping with another woman in the first place.

Maddox made her way outside, wondering a little about where Jessica was off to but caring more about wanting to talk to Avery again. The fire was somehow even brighter than it had been. Of course, Peyton had hired someone to maintain it through the night. Maddox rolled her eyes at her friend. The man who was currently watching the fire burn was actually wearing a Fire Department shirt. He was probably here just to make sure the flames didn't carry into the Southern California winds.

"She thinks of everything," Maddox said to herself.

Then, she looked around to see if she could find Avery. When she did, Maddox noticed she was talking to a man. She squinted since Avery was on the other side of the fire. Was that her brother? He was standing pretty close to be her brother. Maddox walked around the fire to get a better look. That was when she saw the man she'd seen speaking to Avery before, talking to Dario. She recognized Dario from Peyton's tour, but she hadn't ever met Tony. Avery was not talking to her brother. Maddox realized how stupid she had been. She'd assumed that Avery was into women. Why? She had no reason to think that. It had just felt so nice talking to her before. It was comfortable yet exciting at the same time. The way Avery leaned in to listen to something the man was saying, though, was an indicator that she obviously hadn't felt the same way. The woman had just left Maddox in the theater room. That probably meant something. Maddox should have taken the hint. She looked down at the two glasses in her hands, lifted one to her lips, and gulped it down.

CHAPTER 6

"I'M SORRY, what?" Avery asked, leaning in.

"I just asked if you lived nearby," the guy replied.

"Oh, kind of. I'm not exactly living down the beach or anything, but I'm not too far if there's no traffic. Why?" she answered.

He leaned into her ear and said, "I was just thinking that maybe you'd want to get out of here."

"I'm sorry?" she questioned, pulling back.

"I'm not really one for these parties. I only came because my agent told me to. It's a PR thing. If you want, we could go back to your place and ring in the new year together," he suggested. "My hotel isn't too far away, either, so that's an option."

"Are you asking what I think you're asking?"

"You said you came with your brother. You're not here with anyone. I'm not here with anyone. You're sexy as hell," he said, looking her up and down in the most obvious way she'd ever seen.

"I'm not going back to your hotel with you," she replied, taking another step back. "I'm gay."

"What?" he asked, surprised.

"Yeah, I'm a lesbian. So, you're barking up the wrong tree."

"Why didn't you say anything?" the guy asked her, still shocked.

"How is this my fault?" Avery asked. "You came up to me and started talking. I was just listening and being polite. At what point was I supposed to just blurt out that I'm gay?"

"I've clearly been flirting with you this whole time."

"I didn't know that," she returned. "I'll leave you here, so you can find some other woman to flirt with. Maybe she'll take you up on your offer."

Avery walked in the direction where she had seen her brother a few moments before. She found him laughing with Dario. She didn't want to interrupt, but she also didn't really know anyone else here. She worried Tony might get angry with her for getting in the way but hoped that her brother would appreciate that she only came to this party because he'd insisted on it.

"Hey, Avery," Tony said. "Dario, this is my sister, Avery."

"Hello," Dario replied in a thick Italian accent. "It is nice to meet you."

"You too," she said, smiling at him. "I think I'm going to go," she told her brother.

"What? Why?"

"I don't know anyone here, Tony. You clearly don't need me." She nodded slightly toward Dario. "I'd rather just go home and be alone."

"If that's what you want," he said, taking her elbow. "Are you sure, though? It's not even eight yet."

"I'm sure, yeah."

"Happy New Year," Dario told her.

"You too." Avery smiled over at him. "Be smart and be safe," she told her brother, pressing her index finger into his chest.

"Yes, Mom," he teased and gave her his patented wide eyes, which meant it was time for her to leave the two of them alone.

She turned back toward the house and started walking in the deep sand. She really had not dressed for a beach party. Tony should have warned her, but he'd obviously been preoccupied with thoughts of a naked Dario. Had Avery swung that way, she'd understand. Dario was a very attractive man.

"Hey," Maddox said.

"Hi," she replied, meeting Maddox's eyes and giving her an instant smile back.

"Everything okay?" Maddox asked.

"Oh, yeah. I was just heading out."

"You're leaving?" She actually sounded a little sad.

"Well, some actor guy who's been in a few TV movies just asked me to go back to his hotel or my place; whichever was closer."

"Oh." Maddox definitely sounded a little sad now.

"He's kind of a dick," she replied. "We were talking. I was being polite, I thought. He asked me to go ring in the new year with him. What a line, right?"

Maddox laughed a little and said, "You didn't fall for it?"

"No way." Avery laughed. "But he's not exactly my type, either. He got pissed when I told him."

"Told him…"

"That I'm a lesbian," she finished, giving Maddox a shy smile. Maddox nodded a little and held out a glass to her. "Is this to celebrate my lesbianism?"

"No." Maddox shook her head. "I got it for you. I came out here looking for you, saw you talking to him, and figured I'd better just forget about it."

"You got me a drink?" Avery took the glass from her. "That's sweet."

"If you're leaving, though, you probably shouldn't drink that. It's mostly rum, I think. I watched the bartender and didn't stop him when he kept pouring."

"I didn't think I had any reason to stay," Avery replied, taking a sip.

Maddox looked up and down the beach before she asked, "Well, if you'd consider changing your mind, maybe we could take a walk down the beach?"

"Okay. Sure," Avery agreed, surprising herself.

Maddox's smile widened. A waiter came around with a tray. Maddox placed her empty glass on it as he walked past. Avery finished her own drink probably too quickly, especially given what Maddox had told her about the bartender's heavy-handed pour, and did the same. Then, they took off slowly down the beach, thankfully, away from the crowd.

"So, you know I'm a photographer, but what do you do?"

"Oh, it's not nearly as interesting as being a photographer. God, I really didn't dress for a walk on the beach." Avery looked down at her shoes, which were now filled with sand.

"Take them off," Maddox suggested. "Here." She stopped walking, which caused Avery to stop walking, too. Maddox bent down and removed Avery's shoes one at a time. "I hope they weren't expensive." She moved quickly in her bare feet to place them onto one of the many chairs Dani and Peyton must have set up for the night, and returned to her side. "Better?"

"Thank you. Do you think they'll still be there when we walk back?" Avery asked.

"I can't imagine any of their guests stealing a pair of shoes off a beach chair, can you?" Maddox asked back.

"No, I guess not." Avery laughed softly.

"I always take mine off when I come here. I like the feeling of the sand between my toes," Maddox said.

"Really? I've always kind of hated it," she replied.

"But it's like a piece of something, right?" Maddox asked, seemingly excited. "Come here." She took Avery's hand in her own. Avery felt the warmth of it and didn't want to let go. She swallowed as she followed Maddox closer to the ocean. "Water covers so much of this earth. The sand is the thing that binds us to it," she said.

"I guess you're right."

"Want to step in it with me? It's not that cold. I was in it earlier."

"I know. I saw you," Avery said.

Maddox turned to her and asked, "You saw me?"

"You were taking pictures. Then, you rinsed your feet in the water."

"Yeah." Maddox smiled at her.

That smile made Avery feel ten-feet tall, maybe twenty

feet when it was directed at her. Maddox was beautiful. She was nice. Her pictures from earlier tonight showed she was talented. She might just be the complete package.

"So, I'm not a famous photographer or anything."

"Then, what *do* you do?" Maddox smiled at her as they started walking again.

"A couple of years ago, I got this idea for an app."

"An app?"

"Yeah, it's to help people sleep."

"Like a white noise thing?"

"No, it's based on real science," Avery replied. "It keeps track of your circadian rhythm. That's kind of your body's internal time tracker. It tells your body when it's time to be awake and when it's time to go to sleep. I found a way to track it, and in combination with that and a few other things, it can help people sleep a lot better. My tests have shown a forty-eight percent success rate, and I'm only beta testing right now."

"You can help me sleep better with an app? Really? I've tried a few, and I've read all the articles about how to get a better night's sleep, and I still struggle with it most of the time."

"If you download the app and enter in some data on yourself, yeah. It's shown better results in participants who actually went through a full sleep study first and then entered their data, but it's not required. Basically, I'd need to know your height and weight along with some basic health information. You can get some of it from your primary care doctor. Once the information is entered, you start the app right before you try to go to sleep. Then, end it when you start to wake up. You do that for about a month so the app can gather the information it needs to track your rhythm. During the day, you enter some information, too. For example, you tell it when you start to feel tired, when you're energized, and when you eat and drink fluids. Once the app has all the info it needs and it's tracking, it can recommend things like when to turn off any blue light, when to stop eating for the day, or when not to drink coffee or any other kind of caffeine. It'll tell you what time to set your alarm clock for in the morning. It can even suggest if you should listen to white noise or not to drown out other sounds." She smiled at Maddox, who was looking over at her, listening intently. "It'll tell you down to the minute how much time you should spend in the sun; and if you can't get outside, to have one of those UV lights on your desk for a certain amount of time each day. Right now, I'm testing an additional component to the code, which could tell you if you need to take supplements. I'm not a big fan of drugs myself, but supplements like melatonin or lavender have shown they can help people sleep better. I've got a list of about five of those I'm trying to see if the app can recommend. Instead of just telling the user to take a supplement, ideally, it would tell them which one specifically."

"Holy crap, Avery." Maddox laughed as they walked.

"Sorry, I kind of geek out over this stuff."

"Are you a mad scientist or something? Should I be worried you're about to take over the world? Maybe I should be happy. The world's kind of messed up. Can you fix it?" Maddox asked and gave Avery a soft laugh that had Avery's stomach dancing a little.

"I have a Ph.D in computer science, but I'm not a genius or anything," she said.

"You're a doctor?"

"Not a medical one, no."

"But you're still a doctor."

"Yes," Avery answered.

"And how did you get into this whole sleep thing? I mean, photography is an obvious hobby-turned-job. I told you how I got a camera and never stopped taking pictures. What about you?"

"My parents are doctors. My mother is a neurologist. My dad started out as a cardiologist, but he suffered from insomnia, which wasn't ideal for surgery. He started his own practice, and years later, he focused on sleeping disorders. He and my mom work together now, conducting sleep studies and trying to help people sleep better. He was my first guinea pig."

"That's really cool, Avery," Maddox said.

"Testing my app on my father?"

"The whole thing."

"I don't know about cool."

"No, it is. What's the app called? Can I download it now, and you can show me how it works?"

"It's not available in the app stores yet. I'm still working on the overall functionality. Plus, I'd like to get approval from the AMA or the FDA at some point. In order to do that, there are a lot of hoops. Right now, I have money from my parents and a couple of other investors keeping me afloat along with some patients from their practice that have agreed to test it for me."

"And you've done all that in just a couple of years?"

"If you ask my investors, they'll tell you I haven't moved fast enough," she replied.

"Well, I'm happy to be a test subject," Maddox offered.

"Do you really have trouble sleeping?"

"Mostly when I travel; but sometimes, when I'm at home for a while, too. I can't sleep on planes, so that doesn't help."

"My app doesn't have that component yet," Avery said, feeling now less excited.

"What part?"

"Dealing with travel and time zones. I have the code planned out for the next few years. Obviously, that's a big piece of sleep these days, with people traveling for business more and more, but I need to work out some of the easier stuff first. Technically, it will still work. It's just not optimized for that."

"Well, I'm home for the next few weeks. Would that help?"

"You're here for the next few weeks?" she asked, suddenly finding that was much more important than a conversation about her app.

"Yes. Then, Paris, and then Ireland. But didn't you overhear that earlier?"

"Right." Avery laughed and blushed immediately. "I can get you a beta copy of the app if you want. Maybe you could use it when you're home and then when you travel. It would give me some good data, actually." She pulled her phone out of her front sweater pocket – which was the only reason she'd brought the sweater, opened her notes app, and began typing.

"What are you doing?"

"Making notes. If you can test it for even two weeks here to get a good baseline, and then travel to Paris and then to Ireland, I can use that data to see how the app performs when someone's going from time zone to time zone. Can you do it when you get back home, too? That would be even better."

"Sure. Okay," Maddox agreed. "Do you need my phone or–"

"Just your email address. I can email you the file. You'll just download it to your phone."

"Will you walk me through installing it and–"

"It's very user friendly." Avery continued to type. Then, she looked up at Maddox, realizing Maddox was giving her an in. "But yes, I can walk you through it and help you set it up."

"My phone's back in the house." Maddox pointed back at the expansive property. "Do you want to go back now?"

"Can we? Am I ruining your night with this? I wasn't planning on asking anyone here–"

"You are not ruining my night. You're actually kind of making it so far."

Avery smiled and said, "Let's go find your phone and a quiet place to talk then."

CHAPTER 7

"HEY, where were you guys?" Dani asked as they walked along the patio and past the few people who had decided to get into the pool and hot tub.

"Are you drinking vodka straight up, Dani?" Maddox asked her when she noticed the glass of clear liquid in Dani's hand.

"No." She laughed. "It's just water. Did you guys go for a walk?"

"We did," Maddox replied. "Avery wanted to show me something she's been working on. Is it cool if we hang out in one of the guest rooms for a bit?"

"Sure. You can crash here tonight, too, Mad. We figured a few people might need to, at least. Peyton has cars at the ready just in case people want to go home, though, and shouldn't be driving."

"That sounds like Peyton," Maddox said.

"She is the best," Dani replied, smiling.

"Where is she?"

"Inside somewhere. She might be giving a tour. I have no idea. It's best to just let her do her thing at these parties. She loves being the hostess."

"You don't?" Avery asked.

"I do." Dani smiled. "I just miss my daughter. How lame is that? I know this is supposed to be our get-back-out-there party, but I just miss our little girl. This will be the longest we've been away from her. It's only two nights and

46

three days, but it's forever for me. I'm sure she doesn't even miss us and that her grandparents are spoiling her like crazy, but that's why I'm not one hundred percent present tonight. I'm sorry." She shrugged.

"Don't apologize," Maddox said. "You're allowed to miss her."

"I'm going to make sure our friends in the hot tub aren't drinking too much. That can get dangerous," Dani replied. "Once a mom, always a mom, right?" She walked toward the hot tub.

Maddox and Avery continued on their way inside the house, where Maddox caught Peyton talking to Kenzie.

"Hey, Pey?"

"Hey, Mad."

"Is it too late to get your parents on the phone?"

"No, I doubt it. Why?"

"I think Dani's really missing Sienna. Maybe having them FaceTime with you guys for a few minutes will help."

Peyton looked at Maddox first and then outside, where she must have last seen Dani headed. She then smiled at Maddox.

"Thanks, Mad. Kenz, can we–"

"Later, yeah," Kenzie finished.

"Where's Len?" Maddox asked once Peyton had taken off to find her own phone and her wife.

"In the bathroom, I think." Kenzie took a drink from a bottle of water.

"We're going upstairs," Maddox said and took Avery's hand again. "If I see her, do you want me to send her your way?"

"No, I'm good." Kenzie looked around. "But thanks, Maddox," she said softly.

"No problem."

Maddox pulled gently on Avery's hand, enjoying the feel of it in her own and wishing she could entwine their fingers because that would mean Avery was hers. They'd be holding hands walking through this party together, not just as one woman pulling the other through a somewhat crowded hallway toward the stairs.

"Can I ask you something?" Avery said as they now climbed the said stairs.

"Sure."

"Did you ask Kenzie that question because of her Asperger's? Is that wrong to ask?"

Maddox let go of Avery's hand reluctantly as they arrived at the first guest bedroom on the right. She opened the door only to find two people currently making out on the bed.

"Guys, this isn't a high school party. Come on," Maddox said.

"We just needed a moment alone," one of the women said.

"Just make sure that moment doesn't turn into sex on my friend's bed. Understood?" She closed the door. "Can you believe that?"

"Do you know them?" Avery asked.

"No, but two women making out in Peyton and Dani's guest room wasn't what I think Dani had in mind when she said people should make themselves at home."

"Probably not."

They made their way to the next room, which was empty.

"Oh, and yes, to answer your question."

"About Kenzie?"

"Yes, she's awesome. Lennox is great, too, but she married up with that one," Maddox said and offered a wink to show Avery that she was only kidding. "I just check on her sometimes. Parties aren't easy for her."

"I can understand. They're not easy for me, either, but I don't have Asperger's."

"I take it, you've followed them and their relationship online?"

"I know their story, yes, or what they've shared with the world, at least."

"My phone is with my camera. One sec. Don't go anywhere." Maddox held up a finger to indicate she just needed a moment. She then practically ran out of the room, not wanting to risk Avery leaving her again. She made it back quickly and closed the door behind herself, leaving most of the sounds outside their space. "Okay. Here."

"Email?" Avery requested.

Maddox gave her the personal email address she used only with her close friends and family.

"Okay. I just sent the file," Avery told her.

Maddox looked at her phone, saw the notification come in, and they spent the next fifteen minutes installing and customizing the app for her. Maddox sat back on the bed, leaning against the pillows. Avery joined her a few minutes later.

"And I just have to use it now?" Maddox asked.

"Yeah. Tonight is probably a bad night to start, given you'll be up later than you normally are, but I'd say start it the day after tomorrow."

"Why not tomorrow?" She turned her face to Avery.

"You'll probably be sleeping in, and your rhythm will be off. It should be as normal as possible when you start using the app."

"Okay. I'll start it the day after tomorrow, then," she said, lowering her phone between them onto the bed and dropping it there. "It's pretty amazing, what you've created. I could never do that."

"I wouldn't be able to take pictures like you," Avery replied, looking down at her phone. "I just Googled you."

"That's weird. I didn't feel anything," Maddox teased.

"I didn't–" Avery squinted her eyes at her. "Funny."

"*I* thought so," Maddox said, laying her head back further on the pillow, wishing she could fall asleep right here as long as the company she was keeping also stayed and did the same.

"Your photos are remarkable, Maddox Delaney," Avery told her, turning the phone so Maddox could see.

"That's Alaska," she said. "I was there a few years ago. It's gorgeous there. Freezing cold, but gorgeous."

"You've been just about everywhere, haven't you?" Avery asked, placing her phone next to Maddox's on the bed.

"Not everywhere, but I've been to a lot of places. I'm lucky."

"What's one place you still want to go to but haven't yet?" Avery asked.

"Oh, that's a list." Maddox looked over at her. "What about you?"

"I haven't been anywhere."

"Really?"

"Family vacations as a kid. I did Disneyworld and that kind of stuff, but I've never been to the places you've been."

"Well, what's at the top of your list to see?"

"My heritage is Italian. My great-grandparents came here from a little town outside of Naples. So, I guess I'd want to go there and see where I'm from."

Maddox loved that answer. It wasn't just about going to a famous beach or landmark. Avery wanted to find out where her family came from. She wanted to walk the same streets they did and see the sights that once surrounded her ancestors. Maddox had done the same thing when she had found out that she was half French and half English. On one of her many trips, she had gone to the small village in the south of France to see where her father's family came from. On another trip, she went to Southwell, which was north of Nottingham, to see the places her mother's family had seen growing up.

"I've been to Naples a few times. What's the name of the town?"

"Benevento," Avery replied.

"I don't think I've been there. I might have driven through it or something. Maybe I'll go the next time I'm there."

"How often do you just get to go to Naples?" Avery

asked, scooting a little closer to her on the bed.

"I go to Milan for Fashion Week. If I get the chance, I usually stay in Italy after and go exploring with my camera. I've been all over the country. I like Naples because the bay is gorgeous, and you can see Mount Vesuvius in all her dangerous glory."

"It looks beautiful from what I've seen," Avery said.

"Oh, it is," Maddox replied, turning to lie on her side, now facing Avery. "The first time I was there, I–"

The door opened. Maddox and Avery turned to look at who had just disrupted their quiet space.

"Maddie?" Jessica asked.

"Jess, what–"

"Jessica, come on before everyone sees and knows what we're–"

"Lisa?" Maddox said, shooting up from the bed.

Lisa Grandy had her hands on Jessica's hips, holding her from behind as she gave Jess a little push into the room.

"Oh, I guess this one's taken," Lisa replied. "Shit. Mad?"

"Maddie, I didn't know you'd be in here," Jessica said, pushing Lisa's hands off her body. "Who are you?" Jessica asked, looking at Avery now.

"I cannot believe you two." Maddox stood up. "Were you seriously trying to hook up in this room just now?"

"Maddie, you yourself pointed out earlier that we broke up," Jessica said.

"Are you drunk?"

"I'm tipsy. Lisa's drunk."

"Like it matters. It's not like it's our first time," Lisa added, placing her head on Jessica's shoulder. "That was rude, wasn't it?"

"Yes, it was fucking rude," Maddox said. "I haven't seen you since before I found out you were fucking my girlfriend behind my back, Lisa."

"Hey, she wanted me. And I wanted her. It wasn't serious. She loved you. She told me right before *and* after every time I had my hand—"

"Lisa, shut up." Jessica took another step into the room away from her. "I didn't know she was going to be here. She wasn't invited."

"Because Peyton and Dani know what she did."

"I should leave you—"

"No, Avery. Please, stay," Maddox requested as Avery stood.

"Burke called her a couple of hours ago and told her we were here. I didn't know, but then you and I talked, and—I don't know, it just…"

"She showed up, and you decided to fuck her in a guest room while I'm downstairs?"

"You were about to fuck *her* in a guest room with *me* downstairs." Jessica pointed at Avery.

"No, we weren't—"

"Please. You're totally Maddox's type," Jessica said.

"Shut up, Jess. It's not even like that. We were just talking."

"In bed?" Lisa interjected. "Lying down?"

"Yes, Lisa. Some people are capable of just conversing while lying on a bed without fucking someone else's girlfriend."

"This is too intense for me." Lisa held up both hands. "I thought I'd have a quickie and a few more drinks before I went home to pack. I'm flying to New York tomorrow. I don't have time for this bullshit. It's you and your hand tonight, Jess." She then looked at Maddox. "Unless Maddox wants to take you back."

"I'm going downstairs. This really isn't my business," Avery said, slipping past Jessica and Lisa before Maddox could say anything.

Lisa left right after, not bothering to close the door behind them.

"What the actual fuck, Jessica?"

"She just showed up, Maddie. We had a connection back then. When she asked if I wanted to come upstairs, I said yes. I just wanted to get you off my mind."

"And she's done that before, I guess." Maddox grabbed her phone off the bed. "I've got to go."

"Maddox, I told you downstairs that I didn't come here to try to get you back. I got that you don't want me earlier. I only came to try to talk to you and maybe get some closure."

"And fucking Lisa helps you with closure?"

"I had a few too many, and she and I have done this before. She's single. I'm single. You weren't supposed to know about it." Jessica shrugged. "I'm sorry you had to see it. I'm sure it brought back some pretty bad memories for you, but I am allowed to be with other people."

"So am I." Maddox crossed her arms over her chest. "But that didn't stop you from acting like an asshole with Avery."

"I thought you two were just *talking*."

"We *were* just talking, but–"

"You wanted something more? I assume that's why you brought her."

"I didn't bring her. I only just met her tonight," Maddox said. "And I need to go find her. I'm sure she thinks I'm a crazy person after this display."

"Well, I'm sorry for my part in it. I'm going to get a ride and get out of here. I seem to only be causing problems tonight."

"Don't take this the wrong way, Jess, but I kind of hope I don't see you around for a while."

"I get it," she replied. "I'll see about getting Lisa to go home, too. She's pretty drunk already. I don't know if she's going to make it to midnight."

"Is she going home with you?" Maddox asked.

"She might be, Maddie." Jessica shrugged. "She's an asshole when she's drunk, but she's not a bad person. It was my fault, what happened."

"She knew you had a girlfriend then, Jess. She isn't totally innocent."

"Maybe not. But I just dumped the one I found after you, and she was pretty terrible, so maybe Lisa and I were supposed to work all along. I don't know. I do know that I care enough about her to make sure she gets home okay, so I'm going to do that, and call it a year."

Maddox watched her leave the room. She stood still for a moment. She didn't exactly want to run into Jessica or Lisa again, and preferably, ever. She sat at the end of the bed and waited. When she looked down at her phone, staring at the clock on the screen, she decided to give them five minutes before she went back downstairs. Then, she realized that if they could leave in five minutes, Avery could, too.

"Shit," she said to herself.

CHAPTER 8

THE ROOMS were filled with people now. Avery couldn't find a quiet corner to save her life. She thought about sitting down on the sofa in the living room first. There was one empty seat between Lennox and someone she didn't know. She also thought about going back outside, but the patio looked pretty packed through the windows. Then, she thought about finding her brother to get him to give up the idea of sleeping with Dario tonight and spend the new year with his little sister instead. That wasn't right. She decided that maybe this was the end of her first famous people's party. It would likely also be her last famous people's party. The music was louder than before, but that didn't stop her from feeling the vibration of her phone from her sweater pocket.

Assuming it was Tony either checking on her or telling her that he was about to score, she pulled it out to take a look. There was no text message on the screen, though. She unlocked the phone and noticed the notification was for an email. Normally, she wouldn't have bothered, but she had nothing else to do and wanted to appear occupied while she sorted out her thoughts on whether to stay or go; she didn't want anyone else to approach her. For all she knew, the guy from before could come back up to her and make the suggestion that some guys did when they encountered a lesbian they couldn't sleep with. She had heard it all before. And she would probably hear it again, but no, she didn't need to have sex with him or any other guy to prove or disprove she really liked dick.

Avery liked soft skin and even softer lips. She liked the

curve of a woman's hips and the dips that came with it. She liked long hair that she could run her fingers through, and she generally liked it to have a feminine scent; something fruity or floral. She had never before had a specific type when it came to a woman's body or hair color, but when she pictured a woman right now in her mind, she pictured jet-black hair and light-blue eyes. She pictured strong yet feminine-looking calf muscles under capri pants. Avery pictured the soulful expression on a woman's face when she confessed her deepest, darkest secrets. She even pictured tightly closed eyes, flushed skin, and a mouth in the shape of an *O* as that woman came at her touch.

"Maddox," she whispered to herself.

The email from Maddox had come just in time. Avery had been about to give up on this party and the people at it altogether.

"Don't go," Maddox said from behind her, and Avery turned to see her standing there, hands in the back pockets of her pants. "Please."

"Maddox, I don't want to get in the middle of whatever happened up there," she said.

"You're not." Maddox took a step toward her. "Just let me explain, okay?"

"I was just leaving," Avery replied. "I don't fit in here."

"Of course, you do," Maddox said, taking a step toward her.

"Maddox, I'm pretty sure I just ran into your ex-girlfriend – who is a supermodel, by the way, and Lisa Grandy – who is a famous designer. She's so famous, even *I* know who she is."

"Jessica and I aren't together anymore. We haven't been for a while. Tonight was just the first time I've seen her since we ended things, so it was awkward."

"It was *definitely* awkward, but you don't owe me an explanation. We just met tonight. You can do–"

"She cheated on me with Lisa. That's why it was a big deal. Had it been any other woman, it wouldn't have bothered me. It would have just been awkward either way. I mean, do you really like to think about your ex-girlfriends sleeping with other women, let alone see it in person?"

"No, of course not."

"Lisa is part of the reason my relationship ended, but Jess and I are over either way."

"Okay. It's still none of my business, Maddox."

"But what if—"

"Maddox, I'm leaving. It's after nine. If I leave now, I can make it home before all the idiots who decided to drink and drive hit the road."

"Avery, I'm sorry. I don't—"

"It's okay. It was nice meeting you. Happy New Year. I hope you have a good one," she said, biting her tongue because she wanted to say something else.

"You too," Maddox replied, obviously defeated.

Avery wanted to say that she would stay and that they could talk more. She wanted to learn all about Maddox Delaney. Instead, she nodded, turned, and walked down the hall toward the front door. She made it outside into the now-brisk night air and hugged her sweater to her body. She didn't feel drunk, but she had finished that drink Maddox had gotten for her. She shouldn't drive just to be safe. Even though she didn't want to have to come back for her car the next day, she didn't really see a choice. She ordered an Uber and waited out at the curb. It must have been a busy night, which made complete sense given the time of year, because her car took over fifteen minutes to arrive.

She hated to admit it, but every second that ticked by, Avery hoped Maddox would emerge from the house to come and try to get her to go back inside; to implore her to stay and talk more. No such luck. She ended up climbing into the car and watched it drive past her actual car and the party. She made it home in about thirty minutes and walked into her two-bedroom apartment. It was also her office. She didn't have any employees yet since she wanted the money from her investors to go into the work and the product she'd, hopefully, have out to the market soon. Her sister and brother-in-law had moved over an hour away the year prior, which meant she had lost their garage as her office. In a month, she had another investor meeting, and she hadn't even started on her presentation to them, but the intent was to secure her first serious round of funding. Avery had a lot of work to do to make that happen, but tonight was not the night to try to get started.

She dropped her keys onto the small table by her front door and sat down on the sofa in her living room. She had kicked off her now sandy shoes at the door and stared at them, recalling how good it felt to have sand between her toes. It never had before, though. Why had tonight been any different? Oh, it had been different because of Maddox Delaney; that's why. Maddox had been so nice to her tonight. She had brought her a drink, she had listened as Avery rambled on about her work, and she had come after her even after the ordeal with her ex-girlfriend. She'd come after Avery. She hadn't gone after Jessica, the woman she had once dated. Jessica was a beautiful woman. She was a supermodel, of course. Avery had seen her on numerous magazine covers and even in a few makeup commercials. God, Maddox had dated *her*. Nothing had been said between Avery and Maddox about anything other than friendship, or anything other than just two people spending time together at a party, really, but Avery couldn't hold a candle to a woman like that.

Still, she couldn't get it out of her mind. Maddox hadn't gone after Jessica. She hadn't tracked down Lisa Grandy to tell her off for sleeping with her girlfriend at one point. Instead, she had emailed Avery because it was the only way she could think to reach out. Then, she'd found her downstairs and had asked her to stay. Avery recalled the woman's expression when she had told her that she was leaving. Maddox had been sad. She had been disappointed, even. There was something to that, right? What was she supposed to do with that?

She pulled out her phone and opened the browser where she had Googled Maddox. She moved through the images of models, athletes, and nature to images of Maddox herself. Her hair was sometimes up and sometimes down. Her eyes were always gorgeous and light. Her body was, well, in Avery's mind, her body was better than the models and pop stars she was often standing next to in these photos. Avery swallowed hard, remembering the thought she'd had earlier of bringing Maddox to orgasm, and what her body would look like at the very moment the pleasure took over. Just that thought had Avery growing wet, and her clit got hard. When she thought about how good Maddox smelled, and how good the woman's hand had felt in her own, Avery actually spread her legs right there on the sofa and brought her fingers to her sex. She kept them over her underwear, but she pressed two against her body, feeling her swollen clit push back a little.

"Wow," she muttered to herself.

She was ready. She knew she could come right now. All she had to do was apply a few careful strokes, and she'd have an orgasm. She wanted one, too. It had been a long day. Hell, it had been a long year. She could slide her hand inside her panties and stroke herself until she came while she thought about doing the same to Maddox. It would help, right? She couldn't, though, so she removed her hand and closed her legs. She then stood and sighed. She reached for her phone, pulled up the app, and ordered another car. Then, she slid on a different pair of shoes, grabbed her keys, and headed down to meet her ride.

It was after ten when Avery arrived back at the party. She felt completely sober, and as she was contemplating, as she had done the entire ride over, whether or not this was a good idea. She also considered just getting into her car and driving right back home. She shook herself out of that thought as she made her way up the long driveway back to the house. She wondered if Peyton or Dani would answer and wonder why she'd left. She looked to the right and decided to walk around the side of the house instead. She could have sworn she heard the sounds of a couple laughing and, likely, doing something else, too, among the rocks as she passed them, but she didn't plan on stopping to find out. What was it with these people? Didn't most of them own multiple houses they could be having sex in right now? The patio was just as full of people now as it had been when she had left, so Avery went out to the beach where she, surprisingly, found her brother sitting with three other men; Dario among them.

"Hey, I thought you left," Tony said when he saw her approaching.

"Nope," she lied, deciding it was easier to leave that part out of her night. "I thought you would have left by now, too."

"We're sticking around until after midnight," he said. "Then, we're going back to Dario's for the after-party."

"You are welcome to join," Dario told her.

"What?" Avery asked with huge eyes aimed at her brother.

"It's an after-party, Avery. There are going to be a bunch of us there," Tony explained. Then, he stood and leaned in. "But, seriously, don't come over. I plan on taking him to his room as soon as I can and showing him that *I* can be his own personal after-party."

"Gross, Tony," she returned, shoving him backward.

"It might just be," he teased and gave her a wink. "So, have you been having fun?"

"You could say that."

"That's an Avery Simpson non-answer if I ever heard one." Tony crossed his arms over his chest. "Everything okay?"

"Yeah, it's just a lot of people. I didn't think there would be this many people here."

"I didn't, either. Apparently, some people brought more than just a plus one."

"Are Peyton and Dani okay with that?"

"I don't know. I haven't seen either of them since I got out here. I've been a little bit busy." He nodded sideways at Dario, who was in a conversation with the others in the group. Tony pulled her aside. "We made out for like twenty minutes earlier. He's such a good kisser, Avery."

"I'm so happy for you," she said half-seriously and half-sarcastically.

"If you're going to be so salty, you should just go home now. Some of us are enjoying ourselves, little sister."

Avery looked out at the water just past one of the tall torches that had been set up along the shore. She smiled when she saw her. There was definitely something to that.

"I've got to go. Have fun," she said, patting his arm without giving him another look because she didn't want to lose her again.

CHAPTER 9

"I DON'T know, Len. Maybe I'm crazy," Maddox said.

"Because you liked her, and she left?"

"The whole Jessica thing really threw me off," she answered, leaning back on her hands.

"I can't believe she just showed up like that. No way Peyton or Dani invited her."

"They didn't. She came with someone, but she left with Lisa Grandy."

"What? Lisa was here?" Lennox asked.

"I don't know for how long. They're both gone now. I think I'm just going to go home. I told Peyton I'd do the party thing, and I think I did it enough already. I don't really care about ringing in the new year anymore."

"What about Avery?"

"I don't know." Maddox sighed. "I thought we were having a good time, but I might have been misreading things."

"You said you have her email, right?"

"Yeah."

"Email her tomorrow or something. See if she wants to go out for coffee or a drink."

"I guess." Maddox sighed again. "I'm going home. Will you tell Dani and Peyton for me? I don't know where they are."

"Do you have to go?"

The voice came from beside Maddox, who turned to see Avery standing there.

"Hey. I thought you left."

"I did. I kind of came back a few minutes ago." The

woman hooked her thumb behind herself. "I think I might have just heard a couple having sex behind those rocks or something." Avery laughed a little nervously.

Maddox turned instantly to Lennox.

"Hey, it's not us. I'm with you, and Kenz is over there." Lennox pointed at her wife, who was talking to someone by the bonfire. "Oh, I'm going to kill them." Lennox stood then. "They made fun of us for doing that, and those little assholes are totally doing it behind those rocks."

"Who?" Maddox asked.

"Dani and Peyton. It's got to be them. They're the only ones that know about that spot."

"But, they have a bedroom?" Avery pointed out.

"You're not married, are you?" Lennox asked, already knowing the answer. "Sometimes, sex outside the bedroom breaks up the monotony when you've been with someone for a million years."

"So, you and Kenz have monotonous sex?" Maddox teased.

"I could write a book about the kinds of amazing sex I have with my wife, Maddox. You want to read it if I do?"

"What are you talking about?" Kenzie asked them, approaching from behind Lennox and taking her hand.

"Nothing," Lennox replied, laughing a little. "Want to go bust Dani and Peyton with me?"

"Bust them? For what?"

"I'll tell you on the way," Lennox replied, kissing Kenzie's cheek.

"Okay. I guess, bye." She waved at Avery and Maddox as they walked off.

"So, hi again." Avery stood, looking a little nervous.

"Do you want to sit?" Maddox asked, motioning to the large blanket she'd been sharing with Lennox.

"Yeah, okay." Avery sat down next to her but left some space between them.

"So, you were going to leave?" Avery asked her.

"I didn't really have a reason to stay." Maddox shrugged.

"And now?" Avery asked.

"I don't know, to be honest."

"I'm sorry I just left."

"Why did you?"

"I don't know. I didn't really want to come here to begin with." Avery looked out over the water. "Tony convinced me. And all day today, I was thinking about not showing up. I doubt he would have even missed me. He's been with Dario and his other friends all night." She pointed, and Maddox's eyes followed along the beach to find Dario and Tony sitting with some other people she didn't know. "I've spent the better part of two years locked in one small room or another, working on code and science and trying to build something I think can help people and would also make me a lot of money; I'm not completely selfless. It's been a long time since I've been forced to socialize, which is probably at least part of the reason why my brother insisted I come out."

"Forced?"

"That's how it felt earlier in the day."

"And now?"

"I came back, didn't I?"

"You did." Maddox smiled at her. "Why?"

"Because the way I left wasn't fair to you. We'd been having a good time. I didn't want you to think that that wasn't true."

"I'm sorry about Jess."

"Do you want to talk about it?" Avery asked, leaning back on her hands the way Maddox had done earlier.

"Are you cold?" Maddox asked, looking at Avery's legs, which now had goosebumps covering them.

"A little. It's colder than it was when I left."

"Here." Maddox passed another blanket over to her and helped Avery open it. "Peyton thinks of everything, remember?"

"I'm really starting to get that."

In order for them both to get under the blanket, Maddox had to scoot over a bit. She did, and then she leaned back on her hands again, her pinky finger touching Avery's.

"Jess was my first love," she said.

"And she cheated on you? What a bitch."

"She wasn't when we first met," Maddox said. "We were friends before we started dating. My career wasn't crazy big yet. I'd had a couple of gallery shows, but nothing major. It started taking off right when she and I started dating. I just don't think either of us was ready for that."

"She couldn't keep up with it? Was it a jealousy thing?"

"She wasn't out at the time," Maddox explained. "I found out that she was gay when we met. She actually introduced me to the girlfriend I had before her. That relationship only lasted a couple of months. Jess and I used to talk all the time, and eventually, we kissed. She asked if we could keep it a secret, and I agreed. Then, we started dating, and it was amazing for a while. We were together for a long time before I found out about the cheating."

"With Lisa?"

"Yes, with Lisa. They'd been working together. Jessica was the face of her campaign that year. I had no idea it was going on. I was traveling a lot. We did the best we could to make it work with the distance. I even tried phone sex for the first time because of her." Maddox looked over at Avery, who was looking right back at her. "Sorry. That's probably too much information."

Avery laughed and said, "It's okay. Go on."

"Jess claimed that it was my fault. I was the one that was never around. Even when I had the chance to be near her when she had a shoot or a show on location, I had to go somewhere else for a magazine or just for myself. She wasn't totally wrong. I like working in fashion; I feel like I can do some good work there, but my best work is with nature. To take shots of nature, I have to be out in it. I scheduled a few things over some stuff she had, and we couldn't make the connections work."

"I still don't think it's your fault *she* cheated."

"I didn't think so, either, but when we broke up, I started to blame myself a little. I mean, she slept with someone else. I didn't. I've always been completely faithful to whomever I was with. But maybe I shouldn't have taken on those jobs. Maybe I should have followed her to a few extra shoots, just so we could have time together."

"Is her job or her life more important than yours?" Avery asked.

Maddox looked over at her, a little surprised, and said, "No."

"Then, why couldn't she give something up?"

"She's on contract with an agency and with different sponsors and designers. There's only so much say she gets in that stuff. I'm freelance."

"I get that. But I also think there are things to be done when you're unhappy in your relationship before you sleep with someone else," Avery said. "Did she talk to you about how she felt?"

"A little. I thought things were okay, though. The way she talked about it never seemed like it was that bad. There would just be comments about how she wished she could see me more or that we could have more time together, but that's stuff all couples deal with. Then, she *stopped* talking about it. I thought it was over, and we had gotten past it."

"I'm sorry, Maddox."

Maddox looked out at the inky water and said, "It's for the best. Like I said, I'm not still hung up on her or anything. I took her back once before because I'd been very stupid. I'm not doing it again."

"What happened that time?"

"She ended up kissing someone else. She told me it meant nothing. She just missed me again, and I wasn't around. That was the final straw. Tonight was the first time I'd seen her since, though, so that's the only reason I had my momentary freak out up there. I'm sorry you had to see that."

"It's okay. I'm not sure how I would have reacted if my ex and the woman she had cheated on me with would have walked into a bedroom planning to get it on."

"Well, I reacted poorly, and you got caught up in it. I'm sorry. I'm sorry that it caused you to leave." Maddox paused. "But I'm glad that, for whatever reason, you came back."

"Me too." Avery gave her a smile.

"So, enough about me. Let's talk about one of your exes. That will make me feel better," she joked.

"Oh, well, *there's* a topic." Avery sat up, pulling the blanket a little more into her lap. Then, she crossed her legs underneath herself. Maddox knew that even though the blanket was covering her, below it, Avery had only a pair of underwear between her body and the world now. "I don't have very many of them. I'm not sure if that's a good thing or a bad thing."

"I guess that depends on your outlook."

"Well, my most recent relationship was over two years ago. When I got the idea for the app, I kind of got hyper-focused on it. My girlfriend at the time wasn't a fan of me giving up my great job to start my own company and make no money until it was up and running. We hadn't been together long at that time."

"How long?"

"About four months. I wasn't sure I wanted anything long-term at that time anyway, so when she ended it, I didn't argue. I just got back to work. I guess that says something, huh?"

"I guess so."

"But you put up a fight for Jessica. Does that say something, too?" Avery asked as she stared at her own hands in her lap. "I mean, she *is* a famous supermodel. Is that your type? I look around at this party and see only gorgeous women; and then, there's me."

Maddox knew what Avery was asking. She sat up, wiped her hands on her pants to try to get rid of the sweat, and turned her body toward Avery.

"Avery, *you* are gorgeous," she told the woman as she felt her own cheeks flush. "Jessica happens to be a model, but that's not why I fell in love with her. Physical beauty has never mattered to me. I want what's inside a woman. I want someone with a good heart and a good head on her shoulders. Now, if that comes packaged in someone that looks like you, I'm not going to turn it down." Maddox chuckled at her lame attempt at a joke. "You're beautiful, Avery."

Avery didn't say anything for a moment, but she did stretch her legs out in front of her and lie back on the blanket with one arm under her head.

"You're sweet."

Maddox moved a little closer, lying beside her and resting her elbow in the sand. As it sank, she pressed her palm to her head to hold herself up. Then, she pulled the blanket up over them a little more with her free hand before she did something brazen. She placed it on Avery's thigh and kept it still.

"You keep saying I'm being sweet, but I'm not really. I mean what I say when I tell you I think you're beautiful. You're obviously humble. You're pretty damn smart, too. I can't believe you built an app like that all by yourself. That's amazing." Maddox's hand rubbed up and down Avery's thigh without asking for anything as she stared into Avery's eyes. "And, to be clear, you are the best part of my entire day today; maybe even the best part of my year."

"I think that means you've had a pretty terrible year, Maddox." She gasped when Maddox's hand moved a little lower. "I hope that's not the case."

Maddox couldn't see much in the darkness, but she could see the flickering torchlight in Avery's two different-colored eyes, and she could also see the lust building within them.

"It's not. I actually had a great year." Her fingers danced at the hem of Avery's dress. She itched to lift it up and feel her skin. "How was your year?"

"So far, so good." Avery's breathing was coming faster now. "It might get better, though."

"Yeah? What could make it better for you?" Maddox leaned down a little.

Their lips were inches apart now. Maddox slid her hand under the hem and along Avery's thigh, and Avery gasped when she halted at where her thigh met her sex. It was so warm. Avery's skin was so soft. Maddox wanted to touch her. She wanted to kiss Avery.

"I'm happy to help however I can," she added in a whisper.

Then, Maddox let one of her fingers just touch the fabric of Avery's panties, where she knew it would count. Avery's hips lifted on their own slightly. Her eyes showed Maddox that she wanted this. Hell, Maddox wanted this. She needed it. Avery was amazing. After she'd left, Maddox planned to leave, too, but something had told her to stick around for a while. She had no idea what force had been involved in keeping her here, but she was grateful. As she stared into Avery's eyes, she was grateful. She'd gone back outside, pulled out the blanket, and had just stared at the water for a long while as everyone else played and partied around her. Maddox had no interest in the music playing, the booze being consumed, or the food being passed around. She missed Avery. She'd only just met her, but she'd missed her.

"Maddox, we can't out here," Avery said in a whisper.

"No one can see," Maddox replied, sliding her finger along the inside of Avery's thigh. "The blanket is covering up what I'm doing, and no one is looking this way."

"God, I know we should stop," Avery said as she cupped the side of Maddox's face. "We just met. This–"

"Hey, you two." The voice was Peyton's, and it wasn't far away.

CHAPTER 10

MADDOX moved so quickly, Avery worried she had torn her dress. Maddox sat up just as her friends arrived at the blanket. Avery sat up, too, straightened her dress under the blanket to make sure it wasn't torn, and looked up at the four women who had just interrupted an incredibly sexy moment.

"It was totally them, by the way," Lennox said, sitting down next to Maddox on the blanket; apparently, oblivious about what Maddox and Avery had nearly just done.

"What was them?" Maddox asked.

"The rocks."

"Oh," Maddox replied, looking up at Peyton and Dani, who were standing over the blanket. "Really? Guys, you live here."

"We were celebrating," Peyton said, sitting down, too.

Kenzie sat down next to Lennox. Dani sat next to Peyton. That left Maddox and Avery squeezing into the middle between them all. To Avery, it was a little awkward. It felt like she was sitting between five very attractive members of a female pop group or something. It was also awkward because Maddox had just had a hand between her legs with a finger brushing ever so slightly over her clit. She was wet. She was still wet. She had been wet all night thanks to this woman she was currently touching shoulders with due to the lack of space on the blanket now.

"Celebrating what?" Maddox asked.

"Yeah, what were you celebrating? She wouldn't tell us

until we were all together," Lennox said.

"Dani took the test tonight," Peyton said, taking Dani's hand.

"What test?" Kenzie asked.

"You're going to think we're crazy," Peyton said.

Avery didn't know what was going on.

"I'm pregnant again," Dani said.

"What?" Lennox asked.

"You're kidding," Maddox added.

"No, we went through the whole process all over again, and it turns out I'm very fertile," Dani replied.

"I thought you wanted to carry one," Kenzie said to Peyton.

"I do. I still will someday, but Dani loved being pregnant so much. We started talking about our second one pretty much right after Sienna was born. Dani said she wanted to be pregnant again, and I said yes. She took the at-home test tonight."

"That's why she hasn't been drinking," Maddox said.

"I wanted to be careful," Dani replied. "Guys, we're having another baby." She placed her head on Peyton's shoulder.

"I'm so happy for you guys," Lennox said.

"Me too," Kenzie added.

"Are you hoping for a boy or a girl?" Maddox asked.

"Either. It would be cool for Sienna to have a little brother, though."

"I thought you were planning to get back out into modeling, Dani," Lennox said.

"I was, but I don't know that I want that anymore. I've really been loving photography. Maddox has been an awesome teacher. I think I want to go that route for a while. Plus, it keeps me free to go on tour with Peyton whenever I want. We'll be a whole family on tour together."

"Like the Partridge Family?" Lennox asked.

"Sometimes, I forget how much older you are than all of us," Peyton joked.

"I'm not *that* much older than you," Lennox tossed back.

Avery just watched it all.

"What names do you have picked out?" Maddox asked.

"Mad, we literally just got the confirmation that there *is* a baby. We haven't thought about names yet," Peyton said.

"I was thinking Connor if it's a boy and Addison if it's a girl," Dani added.

"You were, were you?" Peyton turned to her wife.

"Well, we had the baby books and stuff. I figured I could flip through them again, just in case I was pregnant. Are they terrible?"

"No, babe." Peyton kissed Dani's temple. "Nothing about this is terrible." Then, Avery heard her whisper into Dani's ear, "I love you so much."

Avery looked away from such an intimate moment between the two women. It seemed like it was something private she shouldn't have seen. At the same time she looked away, though, Maddox looked away, too, and their eyes met. Maddox's light-blue eyes looked amazing in the light from the torches behind and in front of them. Avery didn't want to break the connection between them, but again, she was caught in the moment. It was intimate. It was private. It belonged to them, and no one else should see how Maddox's eyes looked when they were on her tonight.

"So, we're going to keep this between us, okay?" Peyton said. "It's still early, and we'll go to the doctor this week to confirm it, but we don't want it to get out to the public before we're ready."

"No problem," Lennox replied.

Avery turned her head to see Kenzie's head resting on Lennox's shoulder and Lennox's hand running up and down Kenzie's arm.

"When are you two starting?" Dani asked, nodding toward Kenzie and Lennox.

"Yeah, how are our kids supposed to be best friends if they're like a decade apart, Len?" Peyton teased.

"Why are you picking on us? Maddox is right here, too."

Avery felt Maddox get lightly shoved from behind by Lennox because they'd been pressed so closely together. Instinctively, she reached for the woman's forearm to help hold Maddox up. When she let go once Maddox was stable and returned to her position, she met Peyton's eyes and her lifted eyebrow. Then, she saw her smirk.

"You two are married," Maddox said and turned her head toward Kenzie and Lennox. "You should be far ahead of me when it comes to kids."

"You're not getting any younger, Mad."

"Stop trying to deflect on me, Len," Maddox tossed back playfully.

"We should go. We told our families that Dani was taking the test tonight. Everyone's staying up late for the new year, so we should call them and give them something else to celebrate."

"Two of the three trips are here. Are you telling them, Pey?" Lennox asked.

"Peyton's sisters," Maddox whispered into Avery's ear. "Peyton calls them the trips. Two of them are here tonight."

Maddox was that close. The woman's whisper made Avery tingle in all the right places. No, they were all the wrong places. They were in public. She was sharing a blanket with four of Maddox's best friends. They shouldn't have been doing what they'd been about to do on a beach, where anyone could see or, at the very least, hear them because Avery knew they would have heard her loud and clear as she came at Maddox's touch. She was normally pretty quiet in the bedroom, but she had every indication that with Maddox touching her, she would not be. She'd be screaming Maddox's name as she came. The entire neighborhood would have heard her come had Maddox's hand slid inside her panties. Avery would have come completely undone in the best way imaginable.

"Avery?" Maddox said.

"Huh?" She looked around. Everyone was staring at her. "I'm sorry, what?"

"Peyton just asked if things were going well between Tony and Dario," Maddox said.

"Oh." She must have gotten lost in her thoughts of Maddox's hand between her legs. "Yeah, I think so. They're still here. I'm not sure if that's a good thing in the mind of my sex-crazed brother, but they're planning on going back to Dario's place for some after-party."

Avery failed to mention that it was entirely possible that being sex-crazed was a genetic condition because, for the first time in her life, she understood what Tony meant when he told her he needed sex. She had never felt that way until tonight.

"I'm offended," Peyton said. "My party encompasses the after-party. People were supposed to have so much fun that they passed out on the beach or in the guest rooms." She looked over at Dani. "Am I getting so settled with you and the kids that I don't even know how to throw a good party anymore?"

"I love that you just said *kids*," Dani replied. "And you still know how to throw a good party, babe."

"Avery, you're the newest member of the group. Is this a good party? You'll be honest with me, right?"

Maddox cleared her throat.

"Best party I've ever been to," Avery said.

"Are you lying?" Peyton glared at her.

Avery wasn't sure if she should take that glare seriously or not.

"Pey, calm down. Your party is fine." Maddox came to her rescue.

"So, Tony's sister?" Dani changed the subject.

"Yes, that's me," she answered.

"He's an amazing makeup artist. I had him work on me one night when Peyton decided to bring me up on stage.

I had not been prepared for it, but between songs, she rushes off for a quick change, kisses me on the lips, and tells me she's going to call me out on stage to sing the song she wrote for me *to* me."

"Aren't all the love songs about you for Peyton?" Lennox teased.

"Yes, they are. Shut up, Lennox." Peyton laughed.

"Anyway, Tony ran up to my side after he'd finished touching her up and made me look decent. I hadn't even been wearing makeup. I was just there to support my wife. She always likes to keep me on my toes."

"And to think, he had to actually come out of the closet as a teenager. My parents should have known we were both gay. My mom kept buying me makeup, and I never used it. He kept stealing it and would run around the house asking me and our other siblings how his eyeliner looked."

That earned a laugh from the group, which made Avery smile as well.

"How many other siblings do you have?" Peyton asked.

"I have two more besides Tony. He's the oldest. I came next. Then, there were a few relatively peaceful years before our parents had my younger sister, Maria, and younger brother, William."

"And what do they do?" Lennox asked.

"Suddenly, everyone wants to know about me." Avery chuckled through her nervousness.

"You're the only new one. We know everyone else," Dani replied.

"Maria is a nurse. She's married and has a little girl. They just moved about an hour north of LA for her husband's job. William is engaged and is a first-year associate at a law firm in Pasadena."

"And what do you do?"

"She's invented this kick-ass app," Maddox answered for her.

"Kick-ass? What does it do?" Lennox asked.

"It's kind of a long story. I don't want to bother you with it."

But Maddox already had her phone out and the app open. She passed her phone to Peyton and Dani to look at it.

"It can help you sleep better, but it's not one of those junky white noise apps."

"You've seen one of those, you've seen them all." Dani looked at the phone. "What does it do?"

Maddox bumped her shoulder and gave her a sweet smile, encouraging Avery to tell them. So she did. She explained the app, how it worked, how she had gotten the idea because of her parents' work, and her progress so far. They passed Maddox's phone around like they were in a third-grade classroom, and this was show and tell.

"Does it work on pregnant women?" Dani asked.

"Honestly, I hadn't thought about that," Avery replied, pulling out her phone to take the note. "That's not a bad test case, though. Thank you. If I can just pull in the different hormone levels pregnant women experience over the nine months of their pregnancy, I should be able to account for it. You'd have to use it before becoming pregnant, though, probably, to get a good baseline of data, so I'm not entirely sure if I could have the changes actually work for you right now."

Dani and Peyton stared at her when she looked up from her phone.

"You can just do that?" Dani asked.

"Do what?"

"Make something that does what you just said?"

"It's all zeros and ones in the end," she said, shrugging.

"She's a doctor," Maddox added. "She likes to hide that part."

"Doctor?"

"Computer science. I'm not an MD."

Maddox leaned in, and Avery knew what was coming. "Stop diminishing yourself," the woman whispered into Avery's ear. "You're amazing."

"Can I download it?" Lennox asked.

"Me too," Kenzie said.

"She's a terrible sleeper," Lennox added, nodding toward her wife. "Sometimes, she's up three or four times a night, and all I can do is just rub her back to try to get her back to sleep."

"Really?" she asked, turning to face Kenzie.

"Can you walk me through your nighttime routine?" she asked.

"Do you mean when they do or do not have sex?" Peyton asked, chuckling.

"Peyton!" Lennox half-yelled at her best friend.

Then, Avery watched as Lennox pulled Kenzie in protectively. Kenzie blushed a little but seemed otherwise unfazed.

"This is probably a bad topic for a party, huh?" she asked.

"No, it's fine," Kenzie said. "Lennox just gets protective of me sometimes when Peyton's sense of humor is a little too much for me."

"It's been years, and she's still not completely used to me," Peyton said, winking over at Kenzie, who smiled back at her. "Sorry, Kenz."

Then, Avery watched Lennox whisper something into Kenzie's ear. Avery couldn't hear what Lennox said, but she watched as Kenzie's eyes brightened immediately, and her smile got wider. It took a moment for Avery to recognize that Maddox had been whispering in her ear in the same way these couples had been doing. She glanced over at her and gave her a smile. Maddox was so beautiful. She could stare at her all night. Hell, she could stare at her forever.

CHAPTER 11

"So, Avery, huh?" Peyton asked.

"What about her?" Maddox asked back.

"Is it a thing?"

They were standing in line at the downstairs bar, waiting for the bartender to make their drinks. Peyton was getting another champagne and grabbing Dani a Shirley Temple. Maddox was getting herself another drink and grabbing one for Avery, too. After their alone time on the blanket and the long chat with her friends, Maddox needed a drink and a breather. It was just after eleven now. People were starting to feel the new year coming on. Maddox could feel it, too. She could also feel something else. She felt the beat of her heart. She felt the pulse a little lower in her body. She felt good. She felt really, really good.

"What do you mean, is it a thing?"

"You two seemed pretty cozy out there."

"We were, until you guys showed up and interrupted."

"Wait. Really?" Peyton turned to her.

"I…" Maddox looked around and leaned in a little closer to her friend. "I had my hand somewhere it shouldn't have been."

"Maddox!" Peyton exclaimed, and Maddox gave her a glare that told Peyton to quiet down. "Sorry."

Peyton took the two drinks in front of her. Maddox took the other two. Then, Peyton nodded to the side. Maddox followed her into the laundry room, closing the door behind them and placing the glasses on top of the counter next to the washing machine.

"We didn't do anything," Maddox said.

"Spill, Mad." Peyton placed her glasses down on top of the dryer. "You two fooled around on the beach at my party?"

"I just told you nothing happened," Maddox replied.

"But was it about to?"

"I don't know. Maybe." Maddox shrugged and crossed her arms over her chest.

"You just met this girl."

"She's a woman, Peyton, trust me."

"Fine. You just met this *woman.*"

"I did." Maddox looked at her watch. "About five hours ago, I think."

"And you almost slept with her on the beach with all these people around?"

"I think it would have been more just about me touching her quickly to get her off and us making out a lot more than full-on, naked sex on the beach."

"Maddox! You can't just get the girl off on the beach. Is that how you'd really want your first time to be?"

"First time?" Maddox asked and leaned back against the door. "I wasn't thinking about it like that."

"Well, what were you thinking about?"

"How sexy she is. God, Peyton. She's gorgeous, and she's smart as hell. I listened to her talk about her app, and it's so damn cute when she pulls out her phone to take notes. She gets all in her head, and I just want to kiss her. God, I bet she's an amazing kisser."

"Hold on." Peyton held up both hands with her palms aimed at Maddox. "You had your hand down her pants, but you haven't even kissed her yet?"

"She's wearing a dress, Peyton."

"Oh, so you had your hand up her dress, Mad, but you haven't kissed her?"

"It wasn't like that. I wasn't all teenage-boy-like with grabby hands. We were having a nice moment. We've had a lot of nice moments tonight. I was planning on kissing her. I was just holding my hand in place, *behaving*, when her eyes looked so intense. You've seen them, right?"

"Yeah, I've seen them. They're different colors, aren't they?"

"Yeah. One green and one blue. Both amazing. Both incredibly sexy when she's turned on; and she was turned on, Peyton. She was really turned on, and I was turned on, and I kept sliding my hand just a little bit higher, and she didn't stop me."

"What's your endgame, Mad? You planning on going down on her in my theater room while everyone else watches the ball drop and encourages you on? Going to fuck her in the pool with everyone around?"

"Hey, come on. It's not like that."

"This just doesn't seem like you," Peyton replied, crossing her arms now.

"What doesn't seem like me?"

"You're a relationship girl, Mad."

"Yes, I've met myself. I'm well aware what kind of girl I am, Peyton," she replied.

"But you almost hooked up with a woman at the party after only knowing her for–"

"I'm sorry… Just how fast did Lennox and Kenzie hook up after meeting?"

"It wasn't five hours," Peyton replied.

"But it wasn't five days, either."

"That was different."

"Why?"

"Because they were already in love, Mad. I'm no prude. Don't get me wrong. I'm not saying you can't sleep with a woman if that's what you want. I'm just calling attention to the fact that this doesn't seem like you."

"It's not about sex, Peyton."

"Okay." Peyton leaned her side against the washing machine.

"She's special."

"Then, treat her that way, Mad. God, if she's special, you shouldn't be fucking on a blanket with about a hundred people – including her brother – standing around."

"Shit. I hadn't even thought about her brother being there." Maddox smacked her forehead.

"Imagine if he would have walked over while you were… You know." Peyton lifted and lowered her eyebrows quickly. "Is that how you'd want to remember your first time with this special person?"

"No," Maddox replied. "I just wanted to touch her, Pey. I needed to feel her skin. Haven't you ever just needed to touch someone so badly, you couldn't hold back?"

"Yes, I'm married to Dani. Have you seen my hot wife?" she asked, teasing.

"You know what I mean."

"I do. Why do you think we went behind the rocks earlier?" She paused as she seemed to float back in time to earlier that night. "We're crazy for doing this thing again so soon, but Sienna is just so perfect. She's our daughter. I can't imagine loving anyone more than her, but then Dani starts talking about having another one almost right away, and it's like, yes. I want another little Sienna. Your heart just expands, and you're like, I will love our next one as much as I love Sienna. Dani told me she was going to wait to take the test, but then we FaceTimed the grandparents, like you suggested, and they held the phone up to our sleeping daughter, and neither of us could wait until morning."

"So, instead of having sex in your California king, you went outside to do it against some rocks?"

"That wasn't the intention." Peyton rolled her eyes at her. "We wanted to read the results outside. We did that when she took the test for Sienna. It's our good luck charm now. We walked outside with Dani holding a pee stick in her hand. We passed all these people, wished them a happy new year, and walked over to the rocks for some privacy. When she told me it was positive, I couldn't help it. I had to kiss her. Then, I had to be touching her. Then, I had to–"

"Okay. So, you get the idea," Maddox said, stopping her friend from getting too detailed. "Also, you're right. A round against the rocks is great when you've had sex a million times like you two have, but it's not the first time I'd want to have with someone." She sighed. "I just had to touch her." Maddox's head flopped back against the door.

"Damn, girl. You do have it bad."

"She left earlier, and I thought that was it, Pey. I thought I'd lost my shot with this amazing woman, and I'd never really even had a shot to begin with. I've never met anyone I've just instantly clicked with like this."

"She left? When?"

"Yeah, after Jessica and Lisa ruined another moment we were having, she kind of ran out. I thought about chasing her. I *really* thought about chasing her, but… I don't know. Something just told me to let her go."

"Jessica and Lisa? Wait. They're here? What the hell did I miss?"

Maddox filled her in on how she and Avery had been lying on the bed in the guest room talking about where they wanted to travel, and Jessica and Lisa had burst into the room planning on doing a lot more than talking.

"The fuck! I'll kill them."

"I know," Maddox said.

"And Avery just left?"

"Can you blame her? We were having a nice time. I was hoping it would continue. Then, I act like a jealous girlfriend when that's not how I feel. I'm completely over Jessica. I just hadn't been expecting to watch her and Lisa together tonight; or ever."

"I don't blame you."

"I tried to stop her, but it was clear she wanted to go."

"But she's still here?"

"She went home, I guess, but then she came back. She came back, and we were just talking. I was getting to know her; she was getting to know me. And, all of a sudden, she's lying down on that blanket, looking sexy and beautiful, and I kind of went crazy for a minute. Actually, I didn't kind of go crazy. I did go crazy."

"I think there's something to that, Mad."

"What do you mean?"

"I haven't seen you crazy for a woman in a long time. You were crazy about Jessica for a while. I remember that, but this seems, I don't know, different somehow."

"I think I was crazy for Jess because she was my first."

"Your first?" Peyton lifted an eyebrow at her.

"My first love. She was not my first in other ways, if that's what you're getting at."

"So, do you want another first, or do you want an only and forever now, Mad?"

"The latter, please. Do I place my order with you, or do I go straight to Cupid?" she joked. "Seriously, though, Pey. You introduced Lennox and Kenzie, and look at them now."

"I do. I look at them all the time." Peyton smiled. "I love them. They're so happy together. I want them to start popping out babies soon so that little Sienna and either Connor or Addison can have a best friend, but I'll love them even if they decide to remain child-free, too."

"You know Kenzie doesn't want to have them, right?"

"Biologically, she doesn't want to have them because she's afraid they'll be on the spectrum. I know Len has told her that it doesn't matter. Anyway, Len could have them, or they could adopt."

"Do they even want that?"

"I don't know." Peyton threw up her hands. "If you and Avery could just fall madly in love and pop out a couple, then I guess I won't need their kids to be friends with mine."

"How about you just let your kids be friends with the kids they want to be friends with?"

"You're being far too rational, Maddox. I'm already planning to beat up any tiny human that picks on my daughter for any reason, and I'm getting a baseball bat right around the time she turns fourteen. I want to be prepared for when boys come over."

"Or girls?"

"Or girls." Peyton paused at Maddox's glare. "I'm not actually going to hit anyone; I have a security team for that." She pointed at Maddox. "And make no mistake about it, they will follow along to her senior prom to make sure no boy *or* girl tries to pull the shit you just pulled out on the beach. My daughter's first time will not be with some pimply-faced teenager on the sand."

"Hey, I'm not a pimply-faced–"

"But you get the gist."

"I do," Maddox said, laughing. "What do I do, Pey?"

"Go give her that watered-downed drink," Peyton said, nodding toward the glass that was already sweating on the counter. "And talk to her. Just see if you both want the same thing. Who knows? I could be completely wrong. Maybe she *did* want a quickie by the water for her first time with Maddox Delaney; but I doubt it." Peyton paused. "I know Dani mentioned this, too, but there is a guest room with your name on it if you need to stay. She's welcome to stay, too. If something happens up there, just put the sheets in here tomorrow for me." Peyton patted the washing machine next to her.

"I'm not Jessica. I'm not having sex in your guest room, Peyton."

"Why not? You wouldn't be the first," she replied.

CHAPTER 12

"SHE HAD her hand, where exactly?" Tony asked with a lifted eyebrow that Avery guessed was half out of curiosity and half out of protectiveness for his little sister.

"Do you really want to know?" she teased.

"No, but it must be pretty important to your story if you're telling *me* about it. You never talk to me about sex."

"Well, we didn't have sex."

"Thank God. I was like forty feet away, Avery. What if I would have seen her going down on you? I'd have to just walk myself into the ocean weighted down with something."

"She didn't go down on me." Avery laughed at her silly brother.

"You said there was a blanket on top of you two. She could have easily been down there, doing whatever it is you lesbians do to each other." He motioned to her groin area with his pointing and accusing finger.

"I know you know what we do down there," she replied with a lifted eyebrow. "And just because I know it will bug you, I'll tell you it's really fucking good what we do down there."

"Disgusting!" He covered his ears.

Avery laughed at that and said, "Finally getting a taste of your own medicine, aren't you? I still have nightmares about that time you told me you gave your cosmetology school boyfriend a handjob under the dinner table at Thanksgiving. Grandma and Grandpa were there, Tony."

"They didn't see anything, and I made sure he could be quiet."

"You mean, you planned that?"

"No, but he'd always been quiet when he'd—"

"Nope. Never mind." Avery held up her hands and closed her eyes.

"So, where's your girlfriend now?" he asked.

"She's getting us drinks. It's been a minute. The line must be long." She glared at him. "And she's not my girlfriend."

He rolled his eyes and said, "I'll spare you the lesbian stereotype jokes since you've heard them all. Now, tell me. Where was her hand, exactly?"

"Not doing anything I actually wanted it to do, unfortunately." Avery glanced at the sand between her toes, smiling as she thought of Maddox.

"You would have really let her do whatever it was you were doing out here?" he asked, but his voice was more serious, more sincere this time. "Is that like you? I know I love you like crazy, and I like you, too, even though you're my little sister. We're close, Avery. I know you, but we don't talk about your sex life at all. Is that something you do?"

"Sex with someone in public?"

"That and with someone you just met?"

"No, not usually."

"And you were going to do it with her?"

Avery looked at the house to make sure Maddox wasn't anywhere around this conversation.

"I was helpless to resist her," she replied.

"Should I shoot her or something? Is she giving you lines or trying to just get in your pants? I can pretend to be the macho big brother for a night."

Avery laughed and said, "If she wanted to get in my pants, she would have tried something when we were on a bed, lying side by side earlier with no one around at all."

"You were on a bed with her?" he asked a little louder than she'd like.

"Keep your voice down, Tony."

"You were on a bed with her?" he whispered.

"We wanted someplace quiet to talk. I told her all about my app."

"Oh, that explains it." Tony rolled his eyes again.

"Explains what?"

"Why she didn't try to get in your pants then. You bored her to death. Did she actually die and come back to life?"

"Shut up." Avery laughed. "We've had these series of amazing moments all night. Out here, before, we were just talking, and I decided to lie down."

"No reason, right?"

"If you're just going to make fun of me, I'm not telling you the story."

"Fine. Fine."

"She did the same, and then it was like it was just the two of us; no one else was around." Avery thought back to the look in Maddox's eyes. "She was staring down at me, and I was mesmerized by her. I could only see her." She paused and looked out at the water. "And I wanted her. Had we not been interrupted, I would have let her touch me. I know that I would have. I would have kissed her. I would have let her put her hands anywhere she wanted, because I needed her. I've never felt that before."

"That's pretty deep there, little sister." He stared at her earnestly. "You really like this girl as more than just a New Year's Eve hook up, don't you?"

"I think so, yes."

"Does she feel the same way?" he asked.

"I don't know."

"Don't you think you should find out before you two take whatever the next steps are?" He sighed. "You're not me, Avery. I'm reckless. I have one-night stands. I'll probably sleep with Dario tonight, and maybe a few more times if it's any good, but that'll be it for that."

"And you like that?"

"I always have, yes. I like the openness that comes from being single. I like not having to worry about the person waiting at home for me. It's freeing to be able to go where I want, when I want, and be with whomever I want. It turns out Dario understands that better than most."

"What do you mean?"

"He has a boyfriend. He lives in Italy. He comes to visit a few times a year, and Dario goes there whenever he's on a tour and he's nearby."

"You're going to sleep with him when you know this about him?" Avery turned to her big brother, fully prepared to give him a lecture.

"They have an open relationship. He can be with any guy he wants. Dario can do the same. They've even talked about bringing a third into their relationship. They're called thruples or something; three people instead of two. It's an interesting concept."

"Because you'd be able to have threesomes all the time?" she teased.

"Yes," he said and then laughed. "But I think it would be about more than that."

"Wait. Are you seriously considering this?"

"Sleeping with Dario? Yes. I am absolutely going to do that if he wants to later tonight. The other thing? No. I mean, I don't know. I have no idea, really. We've just been talking off and on all night, and he's brought it up a few times. His boyfriend is coming to town in two weeks."

"And?" she asked.

"And maybe I'll meet him or something. Maybe we'll all get it on at Dario's place. Maybe we won't. It might be awesome if we do. It might be terrible. It might be that I like both of them enough to entertain the idea of being involved with them, but I don't know. That's okay for me. I can live in the not knowing. I can live in the gray and be completely and totally happy, Avery. I just don't know that you can. You like your zeros and ones, little sister."

"But, have you seen her eyes? Her lips? Maybe I could

live in the gray for those." She thought back to how close Maddox's lips had been to her own.

"What about her hands? Were those worthy of you living in the gray?"

"Hell, yes." She laughed.

Tony laughed as well and then said, "Well, if you just want the eyes, lips, and hands, I say get yourself a room somewhere tonight and go for it. Maybe you just need to get it out of your system. I mean, how long has it been for you?"

"A while," she said without giving her brother any details.

"There you go. You're probably just horny. Go for it. Live in the gray. Have some fun." He stood. "Just don't do it out here where I can see you, okay?"

"And what if that's not it? What if I want more?"

"Ask the girl out on a date, Avery. If she says yes, great. If she says no, then at least you'll know. Then, you can decide if you want to have your way with her tonight or not."

"Hello," Dario said as he approached and stood next to Tony.

"Hey, Dario," she greeted him from her spot on the blanket.

"So, Phillip and I were wondering if you wanted to go somewhere," Dario said to Tony.

"Where?" Tony asked, turning toward him.

"Over there. Someone told me about these rocks..." He leaned over and whispered something into Tony's ear.

"I'll be right there," Tony smirked. Dario smirked back and walked away. Tony turned to her and said, "Apparently, there are these rocks where people have been hooking up all night. Did you know about this?"

"No clue," she lied.

"Well, he just invited me and this hot studio intern, Phillip, to go over there."

"Both of you, huh?"

"Don't worry. I'll make sure they both get enough

attention from me."

He smirked again as he walked backward in the sand. Then, he promptly fell on his ass after miscalculating a step.

"Be careful. Wouldn't want your uncoordinated issues to get in the way."

Tony stood and wiped the sand off his pants and the back of his shirt.

"I can always just be the bottom."

"Tony, get out of here!" Avery half yelled.

Tony left her alone on the blanket she'd almost had sex on earlier tonight. She looked around for Maddox, who seemed to be taking a long time to bring her a drink. Avery could tell when they had all stood up that Maddox had needed a moment alone, or at least, a moment just with her friends. That was fine by Avery. She'd needed a moment with her only friend here, too. Now, he was going behind rocks with two guys to do things to one another she hoped he would never tell her about. What was it about those rocks?

When she finally saw her, Maddox was talking to a woman Avery recognized but didn't know firsthand. Her name was Ruby Atwell. She was a model and sometimes-actress. She had been on one of those teen dramas as a recurring character for the past few years because she could still pull off looking like a teenager, but Avery knew she was actually thirty-one. She knew that because Ruby Atwell was also one of her big-time Hollywood crushes. The woman had been a model first. Avery remembered seeing her on a commercial and thinking she was cute long before others took notice. She was beautiful. From what Avery had heard, she was also smart. She had taken a career pause to go to Columbia and major in political science. She was also now touching Maddox a little more than was necessary, according to Avery.

Avery watched as Maddox handed Ruby one of the two glasses in her hands. Then, she leaned in and said something into Ruby's ear. Avery balled her hands into fists.

Her nails were short, but she could still feel them digging into her skin. She didn't have the right to be jealous; to feel this way, but she did. Ruby laughed at whatever Maddox said. Her hand went to Maddox's forearm, and it stayed there. Avery swallowed hard as she watched Ruby take a sip from the drink *she* should be drinking from right now. Then, she watched Maddox nod toward the house. They both disappeared inside, and Avery just stood there, wondering if she'd lost her chance.

CHAPTER 13

MADDOX stood at the bar for the second time in the past two minutes.

"So, Jessica wasn't trying to get you back?" Ruby asked.

"She said she wasn't. She said she was just here to talk and try to maybe get some closure or something. I don't know," Maddox replied, taking a sip of her drink.

"Well, that didn't work out well. I can't believe you dated her. You're so much better than her, Mad."

"Thanks, I guess." Maddox chuckled.

"So, what are you doing next?"

"Paris and Ireland," she said.

"Are you doing the Sports Illustrated thing? I thought I heard you were on that one."

"I am, but that's after. I'll be in Bali for about a week."

"I'm going, too," Ruby replied. "They called me up yesterday and asked me. They wanted something with the old guard passing the torch to the new one. They called Dani, too, but she turned them down. I don't know why. I thought she was trying to get back into things now that she's gotten her body back in shape. Not that it needed that much work anyway… She's looking killer, isn't she?"

"Yes, she is," Maddox told her. "And you're not old. Why are you in the old guard?"

"I'm old for modeling, Maddox. Technically, anyone over thirty is old for modeling. Some of us have more staying power than others."

"I guess that's true."

"How have things been since Jess? Are you off the market again?"

"Off the market?" Maddox asked, moving up one spot in line.

"Yeah, you were already taken when we met the first time. Then, you two broke up, but I was with Michael by then. When I ended things with him, you were back with Jessica. I gave you the requisite mourning period, and now I'm coming after you, Maddox Delaney." The woman chuckled at her own comment.

"Wait. What?" Maddox asked, turning toward her. "We're friends, Ruby."

"You were friends with Jess before you got together."

"Right, but I didn't even know you–"

"I wouldn't have gone after you when you were with someone. I'm direct when there's something or someone I want, but I don't go after someone that belongs to someone else."

"So, you're coming after me now?" Maddox checked.

"Are you single?"

"Yes, I–"

"Then, yes. I'm coming after you, Maddox." Ruby stared at Maddox with those dark-brown eyes as they moved one more step in line. "I'd like to start tonight if that's okay with you. It is a great night for first kisses."

"Ruby, I–"

"Do you remember the Labor Day party?"

"You mean, the one hosted by that designer that no one wanted to work with?" Maddox asked, happy for a change in subject.

"Well, I liked you before that, but then I saw you in that bikini, and I couldn't believe Jessica let you go." Ruby leaned in and placed her hand on Maddox's hip. "I thought about asking you out then, but you didn't seem interested in anyone."

"I wasn't."

"Are you now?" Ruby asked.

"I don't know, Ruby. I–"

"Is it a bisexual thing? I have been with women before.

I didn't think you had a problem with it." Ruby pulled back to look at her.

"What? No. I don't. I've dated bisexual women before. I've also dated a couple that never identified as anything. I'm cool with whatever. I just don't know that—"

"Come on, Mad. We've known each other for a couple of years now. I've had a crush on you since we met."

"Really? Why?"

"It's the way you hold that camera." Ruby leaned in again and whispered, "You know exactly where to put it to get your shot."

Maddox cleared her throat at that and moved to stand in front of the bar.

"Rum and Coke," she ordered.

"You have a drink. Why are we even in this line?" Ruby finally asked. "We both have drinks."

"It's not for me or you," Maddox answered.

"Who's it for?" Ruby asked.

"Avery."

"Who's Avery?"

"Ruby, I should grab this and get back out there."

Ruby took a step back and said, "She's waiting for you?"

"Yes."

"You said you were single."

"I am single."

"But, you're going to her?"

"Yes."

"So, there's no chance of me getting a midnight kiss tonight?"

"I'm sure there is. It's just not with me," Maddox replied.

"Well, that's disappointing. I only came here because Dani promised me you'd be here." Ruby looked around the room as if trying to find an escape. "I was going to ask you out and kiss you at midnight. I thought it would be a perfect first kiss kind of moment. We could have grabbed dinner tomorrow night before I have to head back to Toronto to finish shooting the season. I guess I was wrong and stupid for trying to pull off this grand romantic gesture crap."

"I'm sorry, Ruby. I honestly had no idea you felt that way about me. I've been so out of it when it comes to the whole dating and relationship thing," Maddox said.

"No, it's fine. I'll just go find a few people I know here and see if I can get a midnight kiss from someone else. Won't mean the same, but at least it's something. Now that you do know, though – I don't know – if anything changes for you or if you think you might actually feel something for me, maybe give me a call."

Ruby walked off, looking a little defeated, which made Maddox sad. She hadn't had a clue that Ruby had been interested in her. Had she known earlier tonight before she had met Avery, she might have actually entertained the idea of getting to know Ruby in that way. She didn't know, though, and now she never would know if that would have led to something happening between them. And now, that thought didn't really matter. Avery mattered. Getting this drink to her before the stroke of midnight mattered. Around the same time Ruby left her by the bar, Dani nearly walked right past her.

"Dani, hey. Quick but important question for you."

Dani walked over to her with a wide smile on her face. Maddox had seen it there since the moment she and Peyton had revealed their happy news.

"Did you tell Ruby I'd be here?" Maddox asked.

"Oh, yeah. She texted me asking about whether or not you'd be here tonight. I told her you'd be in town and had accepted the invite." Dani stood beside her. "Why?"

"Did you know she wanted to go out with me?"

"Yes, she told me."

"She told you?"

"Yeah, like two years ago and just about every time I've seen her since," Dani said as she chuckled.

"Why didn't you say anything?"

"She asked me not to. But since I just saw her walking away, I guess she told you she's been into you for a while?"

"She did. I was pretty surprised."

"Why? She's pretty much always flirted with you. She was respectful about it when you were with Jessica, but we invited her tonight, and she texted me to ask if you'd be here. I told her you would. She asked if you were single. I told her I was pretty sure you were but that she should check with you because I've been on baby duty and out of the loop, and you've been out of the country a lot. You could have met someone on a shoot." Dani paused as Maddox lifted the glass from the bar and moved out of the line. "What happened between you two?"

"Nothing. She just told me how she felt. I told her I didn't feel the same way. Then, she walked away."

"So, you're not interested in her at all?"

"Avery is waiting outside, Dani."

"I know that, but you met her before you knew Ruby had a thing for you. I didn't know if that changed anything for you."

"Ruby is great. I've always liked her."

"But not like that?"

"I don't know. I've honestly never thought of her that way, but that was because I was with Jess, and she was with Michael."

"I get that. Does what she told you tonight change anything for you, though?"

Maddox looked toward the sliding glass doors as they opened, and a few people came inside.

"Maybe it would have, but Avery's waiting for me," she said.

"You're kind of crazy about her, aren't you?" Dani asked, still smiling, but this time because of Maddox's interest in another woman and not because of her pregnancy.

"I know I just met her, but it's like I met her a long time ago."

"I know the feeling."

"Was it that way for you with Peyton?"

"When I first saw her at that event, she was on stage performing. I thought she was crazy beautiful and so talented, but a few minutes later, when we actually spoke for the first time, I felt like there was no other place on Earth I was supposed to be. My boyfriend, at the time, didn't matter. Lennox being there didn't matter. The crowd all around us – even the people staring at her because she's Peyton Gloss – did not matter. She was the only thing I could see. She swept me away the next morning to Hawaii so I could do a shoot, and I spent the entire time talking to her and sleeping next to her, and I couldn't imagine going home to someone else." She smiled at Maddox even wider than she had been before. "From that moment, the moment I met her, she was the only person I wanted. We had a lot to work out before we could get there, and it was tough. There were moments I thought it wouldn't happen; moments I doubted that it was the right thing to do; moments where I considered just staying with my boyfriend because he wasn't a bad guy and he didn't deserve what I was about to do to him. But she's my one. I had to just accept that and be so happy about it." Her smile widened. "And yes, it was like we knew each other forever, but we'd only just met."

"Do you think it was like that for Kenzie and Lennox too?"

"I don't know. You'd have to ask them. But I have a question for you, too, now."

"What?"

"Why are you trying to compare whatever is going on with you and Avery, to Peyton and I, or to Kenzie and Len?"

"Because you guys are the best couples I know."

"But it's different for everyone, Maddox. I'd hate for you to lose out on something with someone, whether it's Ruby or Avery or someone else entirely, because you're worried about it somehow matching up to what we all experienced when we met."

Maddox noticed Ruby walking toward the front door.

"I'll see you later," she told Dani and hurried, holding on to Avery's drink, toward the door. "Ruby, wait."

Ruby turned and said, "Hey, Mad. I was just leaving."

"Why? What about your midnight kiss?" she asked.

"I was putting on a brave face before." The woman shrugged. "If it's not from you, I don't want it. It was unfair of me to just assume you'd be interested and to come at you like that. Direct has always been my approach, but it's gotten me here to the place where I'm single and basically begging you to kiss me at midnight and go out with me, so I might need to rethink how I go about things like this. I'm sorry. I shouldn't have pulled you into this. I–"

"Ruby, I just wanted to tell you that I do like you."

"But not like that, right?"

"No, not like that. I've always thought of you as a friend, but I've also just met someone. She's outside right now. I hope she's still waiting for me, actually." Maddox laughed softly to try to break the tension. "I just wanted you to know that I do care about you. I want you to find the person for you. I just don't think it's me."

"Well, that sucks, but thanks for being honest, I guess."

"I'm sorry," Maddox replied.

"I'm going to go home and eat some ice cream. I never cheat on my diet, but I think I'm owed one night of wallowing with some rocky road. Happy New Year, Maddox."

"Happy New Year, Ruby," Maddox said softly.

Then, she watched as Ruby left the party.

"What just happened? Didn't Ruby just get here?" Lennox asked.

"She decided to go home instead."

"Oh, she told you," Lennox replied.

"How did you know? Did everyone know but me?"

"That she's into you? Yeah, pretty much. She never officially told me or anything, but Kenzie and I figured it out when she gawked at you at the Labor Day party."

"She gawked?"

"Yeah, you were kind of oblivious about it, but I think you were still dealing with the Jessica thing."

"I had no idea," Maddox said.

"So, you turned her down?"

"Avery," she said as if Lennox needed no more explanation.

"Where *is* Avery?" Lennox asked.

CHAPTER 14

AVERY had watched Maddox talk to Ruby for a few minutes before she had moved over by the pool to sit on one of the chairs there. She knew she had to stay. She couldn't leave the party a second time, and even though Maddox seemed pretty friendly with Ruby Atwell, Avery couldn't leave without saying goodbye. She stared at the partiers who had been brave enough to go swimming at a New Year's Eve party. She wasn't much for pool parties during the summer, but she definitely wasn't getting into this pool, even though it was heated. There were a few guys taking turns on the diving board. Each one tried to outdo the other with a dive. They'd all been drinking. Every dive was terrible. Avery had to laugh at the guy that managed to mess up a cannonball.

There was a couple kissing every so often as they pressed against the side wall of the pool. A woman was on a pool float in the middle of the water, sipping on a drink of some kind. Most of the other people were just sitting in the chairs, talking and having a good time. Avery felt, yet again, that she didn't belong here. That was when she considered leaving again.

"Hi." A woman came up to her chair and sat down in the free one next to it.

"Hey," she greeted.

"I'm Venice."

"Venus?"

"No, Venice." The woman smiled and shook her head. "Don't worry. It happens a lot. My parents got married in

Venice, so they named me after the city. I usually go by my middle name, Valentine. You can call me Val if you want."

"Avery," she said, putting her hand out for Val to shake. "That's a pretty name. Venice Valentine."

"Thanks. Avery's pretty, too."

"Avery Jane. It's pretty basic," she returned.

"You don't seem basic," Val said.

"Oh, no. I am. These shoes are from Target," she revealed.

Val laughed and said, "I've got a couple of pairs from Target, too."

"No, you don't."

"Yes, I do. They're tennis shoes, but they're very comfortable." She looked Avery up and down. "How do you know Dani and Peyton?"

"I don't. Well, I do now. I just didn't before tonight. I came here with my brother, who knows Peyton from her tour. How do you know them?"

"I took a photography class with Dani."

"You're a photographer?" Avery asked, thinking instantly of Maddox.

"No, I took a class. I was dating someone at the time who was in it, and it was a way for us to spend some quality time together," Val said, using air quotes around the word 'quality.'

"He didn't appreciate it?"

"*She* didn't," Val replied.

"I thought lesbian photographers were all the rage," Avery joked.

"Right. Me too," Val said and laughed. "What do you do?"

"She created an app," Maddox said from just behind Avery's chair.

"An app?" Val asked.

"Hey," Avery said to Maddox.

"Hi, sorry it took so long," Maddox said, holding out the rum and Coke for Avery to take. "There was a line."

"No problem," Avery replied. "Maddox, this is Val."

"Hi. Nice to meet you," Val replied.

Maddox moved to sit on the arm of the chair Avery was sitting in. It was a territorial gesture that both annoyed Avery and turned her on at the same time.

"You too. So, what were you two talking about?" Maddox asked.

"She was just asking me what I did for a living. You told her I made an app," Avery said, taking a long drink.

"What do you do?" Maddox asked Val.

"I'm a mere mortal who happened to take a class with a supermodel for a few weeks. I manage a pack and ship store in North Hollywood."

"That's cool." Maddox finished her drink and placed her glass on the small table between the two chairs. "You?"

"I'm one of those lesbian photographers that are all the rage," Maddox replied, wrapping her arm around the back of the chair.

Val watched the movement and said, "Right. I should be going. I have a friend here, and he's probably wondering where I am."

"It was nice to meet you," Maddox said.

"You too." Val looked at Avery. "Avery, have a good rest of your night."

"Happy New Year," Avery replied.

Val stood up and walked away from the pool.

"Sorry, I took so long."

"What the hell was that, Maddox?" Avery stood up, turned around, and looked at her.

"What was what?"

"Your little display just now? The sitting on my chair, wrapping your arm around me, display."

"It wasn't a display. I was just trying to sit close to you. Is that wrong?"

"She was flirting with me, and you didn't like it," Avery said, deciding to put it all out there.

"Okay. So, that's true. I saw it happening when I walked outside, and no, I didn't like it."

"So, you thought you'd come over here and act like an asshole to a nice woman?"

"I didn't act like an asshole. I just asked her questions and answered the ones she asked me."

"You were inside forever, talking to Ruby Atwell, and that's okay, but the moment a woman approaches me, you're allowed to be jealous?"

"Ruby? You saw us talking?"

"Yes, I saw you talking. I know that's what took you so long with the drinks. I almost left again. No way I can compete with two models in one night."

"What are you talking about?" Maddox asked, standing up.

"First, it was Jessica. Now, it's Ruby Atwell. Even *I* had a crush on Ruby Atwell. I mean, we're around the same age, so it's not like I had her poster on my wall or anything, but when she came out a few years ago, I do remember having a few fantasies about meeting her like in a café or something. She'd spill her coffee on me. We'd start talking. She'd buy me a coffee to make it up to me and would offer to pay for my dry cleaning. We'd exchange numbers, and well, you can probably guess what would happen from there."

"You had fantasies about Ruby?"

"Yes, and in none of them was she talking to the woman I'd let feel me up on the beach at a party and getting handsy with her."

Maddox smiled and said, "Ruby and I are friends, Avery. I have a lot of model friends. It's an occupational hazard."

"She didn't seem like a friend to me." Avery crossed her arms over her chest.

"Now, who's jealous?"

"I know I don't have any right to be, but you didn't have the right to basically get rid of Val before."

"You're right. I didn't." Maddox looked around and nodded. "She's over there. If you want, I can leave you alone. You can go talk to her."

"I don't want to talk to her. I want to talk to you."

"Then, let's talk."

Avery looked around and said, "It's too crowded here."

"Do you want to leave the party?" Maddox asked. "There's a diner about ten minutes from here. We can get some coffee and just talk."

"No, it's almost midnight. We should stay."

"Back to the beach?"

"No, I'm pretty sure my brother is having sex out there somewhere."

"Gross," Maddox said.

"Tell me about it," Avery replied, chuckling, feeling a little of the tension leave her.

"I have kind of a strange idea." Maddox lifted her eyebrow.

"Strange idea?"

"It's the one room in this house I know Dani and Peyton won't let *anyone* go into."

"Then, how will we–"

"Don't worry about that. Just grab us some food and maybe some water. I don't think I should have another drink. That one's starting to go to my head already. I'll talk to Peyton or Dani. Meet me in the game room in, like, five minutes?"

"Okay. This is weird. You know that, right?"

"Yes." Maddox laughed. "Just trust me, okay?"

Avery nodded, and Maddox walked off. Avery waited a moment before she headed into the house and grabbed two plates of appetizers, some vegetables and fruit from a giant platter, and some pretzels. Then, she grabbed a couple of bottles of water that she stuffed into the pockets of her sweater and walked up the stairs. She went into the game room and watched the people playing pool for a moment.

Finally, Maddox came to the doorway and nodded to the side for Avery to follow. Avery walked behind her down the hallway up to the third floor, where Maddox held up a key.

"What do we need a key to?"

"Sienna's playroom," Maddox said as she unlocked the room with the key and opened the door.

"Maddox, we shouldn't be in here."

"Peyton gave me the key."

"What did you tell her?"

"That we wanted somewhere to talk, and that I didn't think it should be a guest room with a giant bed since that didn't work out so well the first time."

"And it's just okay that we're in her daughter's playroom?"

"Sienna's a baby. She hasn't even used this room yet. Peyton and Dani just have it ready for her for when she's old enough. Dani showed me when they finished it, and I thought it would be a nice, peaceful place to talk." Maddox locked the door behind them. "Now, there can be no interruptions."

"You really thought this out, didn't you?"

"As of about five minutes ago, yes." Maddox laughed. "Look." She nodded in the direction of what looked like a loft above those multi-colored puzzle floor coverings. "Pretty cool, huh?"

Under the loft, there were already shelves of books lining the wall and a beanbag chair in front of them. The rest of the room was filled with toys and a small, pink tent.

"They really are planners, aren't they?"

"They were just really excited to be parents. Peyton started on this room almost right away."

"It's beautiful. I'm sure Sienna will love it."

"Me too. Come up here with me." Maddox motioned with her hand toward the ladder that led up to the loft.

"Is that made for two adults?"

"Yes, it's been tested. They wanted to make sure they could both be up there with her. You can trust it." Maddox began climbing the ladder. "And it's not like those lame lofts in college, either. It's actually wide enough for two people to lie on with some room between."

"Yeah? Who did you have to squeeze into a twin bed with in college?" Avery climbed up the ladder.

"Breanna Galloway," Maddox replied as she helped Avery get up to the loft. "We were both taking art history. She asked if she could borrow a piece of paper. I asked if she planned to give it back. We ended up making out in a bowling alley arcade two nights later. After that, we went back to my dorm. My roommate wasn't there, so we took advantage of the situation."

"How old were you?" Avery asked.

"I was a sophomore," Maddox asked. "What about you? Who shared your twin bed in college?"

"Well, I lived at home for the first two years to save money. My parents didn't help with school. They said it was important we all learn to pay our own way, but they did let us live at home rent-free to help with expenses. I didn't move out until my junior year with my friend. We shared a one-bedroom, though, because it was all we could afford."

"So, you *did* have a twin bed?"

"I did." Avery laughed as she settled with her feet under her. "And I ended up not needing to worry about my roommate being there or not because I shared the twin bed with said roommate."

"You did, huh?"

"I did. We dated for about six months after that."

"Why'd you break up?" Maddox asked.

"Because she was a year older than me and had gotten into grad school in Texas. We weren't crazy in love or anything, so we just ended it when she moved out."

"Who was your first love then?"

"What do you mean?"

"You said you two weren't crazy in love. Who was your first love?"

"Oh, I guess that would be Marissa Metcalfe."

"That sounds like the girlfriend of a superhero," Maddox said.

"She definitely wasn't a superhero's girlfriend," Avery replied.

"What's that mean?" Maddox leaned against the back wall.

"She was one of the rebellious girls with the emo vibe."

"You fell for an emo girl?" Maddox chuckled.

"I did. She wore all black. Well, sometimes, there was gray mixed in. She had a nose ring, a tongue ring, and pierced nipples. She listened to goth rock – which is a genre I didn't know existed – and she was abrasive to everyone in the world but me."

"Really?"

"Yeah, we had PE together, and I hated gym class, so I usually lied about being on my period or being sick so that I didn't have to participate. She pretty much pulled the same crap. We ended up talking one day as we sat on the bleachers. We did that a few times before we hung out after school. One thing led to another, and we ended up lying in her bed kissing one afternoon."

"So, she was your first?"

"She was," Avery answered.

"When did you guys end?"

"We ended like most high school relationships do. We tried to keep it together during the summer between senior year and college, but the fact that she was going to school far away made us both feel depressed. It got hard after that, and we decided to end things about two months into freshman year at college. She told me later that she'd been seeing someone from her LGBT group on campus while we were dating, but that was the summer after when she returned home from school. I was over it by then, so it didn't bother me."

"You mean it didn't bother you how Jess and Lisa bothered me tonight?"

CHAPTER 15

MADDOX knew she shouldn't have asked that question. It only brought Jessica back up into a conversation she only wanted to be about getting to know Avery better.

"I don't think it's the same, actually," Avery replied, leaning back against the other wall that lined the side of the room.

"You don't?"

"No, for starters, it was high school and college. She was my first love, but I don't know that it was really love; at least, not the adult kind of love, where you have to pay your own bills, do your own laundry, and then deal with the conversations you have when you're a teenager."

"Like what?" Maddox asked, finding Avery's thoughts endlessly interesting.

"Well, in high school, you can talk about if you want to get married and have kids, where you want to live, and what you want to do for a living. When you're an adult, you're not just *talking* about those things anymore. You're *living* them. You're planning on the kids, or you're not. You're moving to that city, or you're not. Marissa and I only got to the talking phase. She's living out the decisions with someone else."

"Who?"

"Oh, I don't know. I don't mean that I know she's with someone. I just assume. Most people our age are married with kids or married and about to have kids or just in serious relationships."

"Except for you and me."

"That is what it feels like sometimes, isn't it?" Avery let out an exasperated sigh.

"Yes, it is," Maddox answered. "And I really am sorry about what I did by the pool. I don't think I realized I was doing it until after I actually did it, but I get how that came off to you and probably to her."

"Can I confess something?" Avery asked, offering a smile.

"Yes." Maddox smiled back at her.

"It was kind of hot," Avery said.

"It was?"

"Yeah, it was like you were claiming me as your own or something. I mean, maybe you weren't, but it felt that way to me."

"Trust me, when I claim you, you'll know," Maddox said before she could think too much about it. "So, are you hungry?" She cleared her throat and changed the subject the moment she felt the blush creep up her cheeks. "You brought quite a spread."

"Yes, and I can't believe we managed to get it up here without dropping anything or making a mess."

"I haven't eaten anything all night," Maddox said, reaching for a carrot stick. "Which is probably why I feel tipsy right now."

"Me too," Avery replied.

They were silent for a few minutes while they snacked. Maddox hadn't realized how hungry she was until she started eating. She finished everything on one of the plates and felt terrible until she looked at the other plate and noticed how empty it was.

"I needed that." Maddox leaned back again. She looked over at Avery, who was taking a drink of her water. "So, about earlier."

"The pool earlier, the beach earlier, the bedroom earlier, or the theater earlier?" Avery asked.

"We've been in just about every room of this house,

haven't we?" Maddox asked through a wide smile. "But I was talking about the beach."

"Oh," Avery said as she visibly swallowed and stared at Maddox.

Maddox waited on her to add something else, but she didn't. They stared at one another for a long moment. Maddox looked into those green and blue eyes before she lowered her gaze to Avery's lips, wanting nothing more than to just kiss them, lay Avery down, and make love to her.

"I need to apologize for that, too," Maddox said.

"Why? It's not like I stopped you."

Maddox gulped and said, "I know, but that's not how it should happen between us. I mean, if it happens at all. I'm not saying it will. Just that if it does, it–"

"Shouldn't be on the beach in the middle of the party where my brother is standing on the other side of a bonfire?" Avery interjected.

"Exactly." Maddox nodded solemnly. "Again, I'm very sorry."

"We were both there, and I didn't push your hand away, Maddox. It's my fault, too. So, I'm sorry."

"Would you have?" Maddox asked.

"Would I have what?"

"Stopped me," Maddox said before she swallowed. "If we weren't interrupted, would we have…"

"Had sex on the beach with people around?"

"Yes," she replied.

"I don't know." Avery sighed and leaned against the wall again. "Part of me says yes, we would have."

"And the other part?"

"Hopes that I would have stopped you," she replied.

"Got it." Maddox nodded. "Can I ask why? I mean, I get it. I guess I just wanted to–"

"Because it wouldn't have been right."

"Right."

"It would have been good, though," Avery said, softening the blow.

"Yeah?" Maddox asked with a lifted eyebrow.

"I think so. It felt good what you were doing, and you hadn't really done anything yet. I did want it. Just to be clear. It felt very, very good, Maddox," Avery replied honestly.

"It did feel good," Maddox agreed.

Avery laughed a little and asked, "Where do we go from here?"

"That's a good question," Maddox said. "I was wrong earlier with the pool thing. If you want to go back down and talk to her, I'll understand."

"What? No, I don't want that. I want to talk to you," Avery replied. Maddox stretched out her legs on the loft. Avery picked up Maddox's calves, extended her own legs, and put Maddox's on top of her thighs. "I want to stay here and continue whatever this is."

"Well, you are trapped by my legs now, so there's no way out for you anyway," she joked.

"Clearly, I live here now," Avery joked back.

"Not a bad place to live. There's usually good food, and there are a ton of toys," Maddox continued.

"Hey, Maddox?" Avery said in a not joking tone.

"Yeah?"

"Do you want to maybe just keep talking for a while?"

"Yeah, I would love that," Maddox said, smiling at her.

"Okay. Me too. Where do we start?"

"Birth, I think." She laughed. "Where were you born?"

"Oh, wow." Avery laughed. "Here. I'm actually a Los Angeles native. You?"

"Bakersfield, but we moved here when I was about three."

"Siblings?"

"I have a younger brother," Maddox said. "And you have three, right? Tony, Maria, and William?"

"You remember that?"

"I do," Maddox confirmed.

"They got two gays in a row with Tony and me. I think they were both a little concerned up until Maria got hitched." Avery laughed. "Even I was a little concerned about that one. She had a very, very close friend growing up. I wondered if there was something else to that."

"You never asked?" Maddox asked.

"No. I love my little sister, but Tony and I were always close. She's closer to William. It's probably just the gap in ages. I don't want to ask now because it doesn't matter. She's happy and in love."

"That's good."

"It is, yes. Will is the only one I was certain was completely straight. That boy is the very definition of a straight guy."

"You'd be surprised," Maddox said.

"I guess it's always possible, huh?" Avery asked.

"How did your parents take you coming out?"

"Well." Avery shrugged. "I'm not sure if it helped or harmed me that Tony came out first."

"Was *he* helpful?"

"He was, yeah. I told him long before I told anyone else. I started thinking about my sexuality in my early teens but was still questioning by the time he came out."

"What about that first love?"

"No one knew about her." Avery placed her hands on Maddox's calves, stilling them there. "She didn't want anyone to know, either. We pretended we were friends. We spent the night together as friends. By the time we actually started having sex, our families all just assumed we were just sleeping. It worked out really well for us."

"You little rebel, you," Maddox teased.

"When she left, it didn't make sense to confess it to them then, so that's why I waited until college. I was still dating guys, too, though. I think I was trying to figure out if I was only attracted to women or if I could be attracted to men, too. I had a boyfriend after Marissa. He was great. I just wasn't into him like I was with her. Then, I had to figure out if it was just him or all guys."

"How did you figure it out?"

"I had to be honest with myself. Sex with him was never how it was with her, and it wasn't just because I was in love with her, and I never got there with him. I never got there with him because I'm gay. I just needed to admit it to myself. Then, I was able to tell my parents. By that time, Tony had been out for a few years. I do think they were worried that their genes had somehow combined to make four out of four kids gay, but not in a bad way like they were going to disown us. They just didn't want us to have to go through what being different means in this world, usually."

"I can understand that. If I ever have kids, I hope the world changes enough to let them be who they are regardless of what that is."

"Oh, there's an interesting topic," Avery said with a chuckle.

"You want to talk kids with me, Avery Jane?" Maddox teased, reaching forward to pinch Avery's arm through her sweater.

"You overheard me telling her my middle name, too?"

"I did," Maddox confessed. "Sorry." She shrugged a shoulder.

"It's fine, and I think we should get married first. I'm pretty old-fashioned like that," she said.

"Is that a proposal?" Maddox teased back.

"Do you *want* it to be a proposal?"

What was Maddox supposed to say to that? She gulped, hoping the music that was barely audible in the room was loud enough to drown out the sound of it. Avery's mesmerizing eyes were locked on her own, and Maddox felt her throat grow dry while another place got wet. Avery's eyes darkened, and Maddox knew they needed to change the subject or get out of this room. She wasn't about to make out with a woman or do something more in a room built for a toddler, and her best friend's toddler at that. Since when did she get turned on at the idea of marriage? She had thought of getting married before, sure. It sounded nice. She wanted the wife and the kids one day.

But the thought of doing that all with Jessica hadn't ever made her go weak in the knees or wet between her thighs. She swallowed again, causing her dry throat to go scratchy.

"Maybe we can save the proposal for later," Maddox suggested after a long moment.

"Maybe," Avery replied, smiling.

CHAPTER 16

AVERY had no idea what was going on. They'd been locked away in a kid's room for a while now. She hadn't checked her phone for the time, but she knew it was getting close to midnight. It was like this ever-present thought in her mind. What would happen at midnight? Would they count down together? Would Maddox sit up, lean in, and kiss her? Should Avery kiss her instead? What if they kiss, and they don't want to stop? Would they just have sex on this loft made for a tiny human? No, they couldn't do that. Avery would never be able to look at Peyton and Dani the same way again if they did that.

That was weird. At some point during this very long day and now night, she'd started referring to them as just Peyton and Dani, and not Peyton Gloss and Dani Wilder. When had that happened? What did that mean? Was she now friends with Peyton Gloss and Dani Wilder? No, they were Peyton and Dani now, and this was their daughter's room. She was in Dani and Peyton's daughter's room with a beautiful woman she had only just met who she couldn't stop making sex-eyes at. Seriously, she had to stop making sex-eyes at Maddox Delaney. Maddox was making sex-eyes at her, too, though. It was obvious what they both wanted to happen. They had been flirting all night. Everything was palpable now. Avery had her fingers sliding up and down Maddox's legs, sometimes drawing lazy circles on her knees. Maddox's eyes were closed, and her head was back against the wall.

"Probably gray," Maddox said.

"Gray is your favorite color? Really? You've got to be the first person ever to have gray as a favorite color," Avery told her.

They'd been exchanging favorite and least favorite things for the past few minutes. It had helped take their minds off the other conversations they had had thus far, which seem to have turned them both on and gotten them ready to go.

"I'm a photographer. I love black-and-white photos," Maddox began. "I think it kind of does them a disservice calling them that though. I mean, they are black and white, but there are a million shades of gray in there, too. I love editing them, looking at them, trying to bring out the elements of the photo that would really make it pop without messing with the integrity of the picture. I think we all live our lives in the shades. Things are rarely just black or white."

"That's pretty deep," Avery said softly.

"Well, I'm tired. I guess I get philosophical when I'm exhausted."

"Do you want to go to sleep?" Avery asked, sliding her fingers just a little higher up Maddox's clothes-covered leg, wishing she could just touch the skin beneath.

"You're putting me to sleep now," Maddox replied. "Seriously, I could fall asleep from you doing that. It feels really good."

She had yet to open her eyes. Avery just stared at her, wanting to move next to her, lie down beside her, and wrap her arms around this woman.

"I should stop then," Avery said, stopping her hands.

"Why?" Maddox's eyes opened.

"Because I'm selfish." She shrugged. "I don't want you to fall asleep. I want to keep talking to you."

"Then, I should go splash some water on my face or something." Maddox sat up. "It's so close to the damn new year, but I might not make it if I don't stand up."

"How about we take a break? We can go to the bathroom. I know there's more than one on this floor. You do that, I'll freshen up myself, and we can meet back here," she suggested.

"Deal," Maddox replied.

Maddox lifted her legs off Avery's lap. Avery had to climb down the ladder first due to her proximity to that part of the loft. When she made it to the ground, she turned instinctively to see if Maddox needed any help. She didn't, but when Maddox turned around, they were face to face. Their lips were mere inches away. Avery wanted so badly to kiss her, but that internal clock was telling her that the first kiss with Maddox Delaney should not be rushed, and Avery really had to pee.

"I'll see you back here?" she asked instead, taking a step back.

"Yeah," Maddox replied softly, obviously realizing their proximity and walking around Avery to unlock and open the door. "After you." She motioned for Avery to leave first.

When they were out in the hall, the music was louder. There were only a few people on this floor, and most weren't down at this end of the hall. Avery headed toward the first bathroom and then looked over at Maddox, who nodded toward that door, meaning Avery should take it, and she'd find another. Avery went inside, took care of that pressing need, and washed her hands. Then, she stared at herself in the mirror for a long moment. She straightened her now somewhat wrinkled dress, wiped at some sand that had stubbornly stuck to the sides of her ankles, and decided to remove her sweater. Then, she looked at herself again. No, she needed the sweater. Her bra was thin, and her nipples were peeking out through the dress. It wasn't due to the cold, either. Maddox turned her on in a way no other woman had before. Her eyes were light but intense. Her smile was genuine. Her smirk was sexy as hell. Maddox's legs were strong. Her stomach looked flat, but Avery hadn't felt it yet. Her arms were toned, likely from lifting heavy camera equipment. God, Avery even found her cute button nose adorable. She wanted to both stare at her with an expression of awe and fuck her senseless.

"Jesus," she said to herself. "I want her," she added, for no reason other than to say it out loud for the first time. "I really, really want her."

Her panties were wet. They had been since long before she'd taken that Uber home and felt for herself how turned on she was. She thought about taking care of it right now. She knew she'd come quickly. Then, she could go out and keep talking to Maddox without at least the need of that first orgasm occupying every single thought. She could have one right now, get through the rest of the party, see where things went with Maddox, and go home to find her vibrator or dildo and have a solo round or two and three if she needed it. And, God, did she think she'd need it. She pressed her palms to her breasts, feeling them full from desire, and used her forefingers and thumbs to roll her nipples, closing her eyes to enjoy the sensations. Then, she lowered one hand to lift the hem of her dress. Standing right there in the middle of Dani Wilder and Peyton Gloss's third-floor bathroom, she lifted her dress on one side and slid her hand inside her panties.

"Oh, yes," she whispered to herself.

Her clit was harder than before. It was swollen and ready, and all she had to do was stroke it just right. As she slid two fingers inside herself, bringing her desire with her to coat her needy clit, there was a knock at the door. Her hand shot out of her panties. She cursed under her breath. Then, she straightened her dress and turned the water on quickly to wash her hand.

"Anyone in there? The downstairs bathrooms are full," a voice said.

"Just a minute," she replied through the door.

She finished up, tried her best not to look horny and frustrated because she hadn't been able to finish, and opened the door.

"Oh, hi," Val said.

"Hey," Avery replied.

"Sorry, I didn't know it was you," Val said.

"It's okay. Go ahead," she replied, motioning for Val to go into the bathroom as she exited.

"Hey, can you wait a second?" Val asked as she walked past her.

"Oh, sure," Avery said.

"Cool. Just one minute." She held up a finger and smiled at her before she closed the bathroom door between them.

Avery had no idea what she was waiting for, but it didn't matter, really. Maddox would be back in a second, and she would have to walk past them to get to Sienna's room, so waiting for her here made sense. They had locked Sienna's door per Peyton's request when Maddox had asked for the key, so she couldn't get back in until the woman returned anyway.

"Hi," Avery said when Val opened the door.

"Hey, thanks for waiting."

"Sure. What's up?" Avery asked, closing her arms over her chest because her rock-hard nipples might just be so hard now that Val could see them through the sweater, too.

"Are you with her?" Val asked.

"I'm sorry?"

"Maddox Delaney; are you two together?"

"Oh, no," she answered honestly. "We met tonight."

"Really? It kind of seemed like you two were here together."

"We're getting to know one another," Avery said. "We've been spending a lot of time together tonight."

"So, that's what I was picking up on at the pool?"

"Probably," she said.

"She was pretty protective there, staking her claim on you." Val chuckled as she leaned against the other wall opposite Avery.

"She was, wasn't she?" Avery said, laughing a little. "I thought it was kind of cute."

"I can see that from *your* perspective, yeah." Val smiled at her. "I thought it was a little aggressive, but that's because I was trying to flirt with you."

"You were? Really?"

She wasn't oblivious or naïve; Avery knew when she was being flirted with. She had just never had so many potential suitors in one night in her life; in one year, even. The idea that Maddox was interested in her at the same time Val wanted to flirt with her, was a lot for Avery to process. At least the guy on the beach could be tossed out of the processing entirely, though.

"Yes. It wasn't obvious?" the woman asked with flushed cheeks.

"I don't know. Tonight has been a weird night for me. You could have just been striking up a conversation with a lonely-looking woman by the pool who had no one else to talk to."

"You didn't look lonely to me. You looked kind of cute," Val replied.

"Oh, thank you," she said, surprised.

"So, you and Maddox are *not* together?"

Avery bit her lower lip, trying to figure out how to answer that exactly. They weren't technically together. They had been talking on and off all night, but that hardly meant they were dating, let alone were girlfriends. They had joked about proposals, but that was about the extent of their talking on what tonight meant to both of them, if anything at all. No, that was dumb. It meant something to both of them. Avery knew that. She needed to trust her instincts here and not be stupid. She'd be honest with Val because whatever Val had in mind wasn't going to happen.

"We're not actually together, no, but I–"

"Great. Any chance you would want to grab a drink with me? I know tonight's weird because we're at this giant party, but we could grab one now, talk a little bit, and if it goes well, I could maybe take you out sometime. This party is nice, but dinner, I think, would be nicer."

"What I meant was that we're not together, but I really, really like her," Avery replied, trying not to be deterred due to Val's interruption. "I've never met anyone like Maddox, and I'd like to see where it goes," she added.

"I can understand that, but that doesn't mean you can't have a drink with me, too, right?"

"Technically, no. But I want to spend the rest of this party getting to know her. I'm sorry. I know that sounds rude. It's just, I'm not great with flirting or dating. I haven't done it in a while. I'm not used to this much attention, and I think I'd like to see what happens with Maddox. To do that, I need to put my full attention there. I'm not great with dating multiple people, and – I don't know – I just think there's something with her I need to pursue. I'm sorry."

"No, it's okay. I'm bouncing back from a bad breakup. Just trying to put myself out there again, so I'm probably doing this all wrong. I'm not usually this forward."

"I didn't think you were being forward," Avery replied.

"Well, yeah, I guess that's true. You did have no idea I was flirting with you downstairs." Val chuckled, likely to reduce some of the tension between them.

"If I hadn't met Maddox earlier tonight, I'd have that drink with you, Val."

"Rubbing salt in the wound there, Avery?" Val teased.

"Sorry, I just meant that you seem nice. I think we would still be talking down there by the pool, but when she came up to us and just…"

"Staked her claim?" Val finished for her. "Basically, peed on you to mark her territory?"

Avery laughed and said, "Yes."

"You liked it," Val stated.

"God, yes," Avery let out in a husky voice.

"Oh. You, like, *really* liked it," Val added. "Like, you were thinking about her naked because you liked it so much."

"Yes." Avery laughed again. "I swear, I'm not usually like this."

"You really do like her, huh?" Val asked.

"I do." Avery smiled dreamily. "I saw her on the beach with her camera, and even though I couldn't make anything out about her, I just knew I'd like her. Is that weird?"

"I don't think so. It happens sometimes. It happened with my last girlfriend."

"The one you just broke up with?" Avery asked, making small talk because she hadn't seen Maddox yet.

"Yeah. Her name is Kristina, and I wanted to marry her."

"What happened? I mean, if you don't mind me asking." Avery glanced toward the stairway again, checking for Maddox.

"We just grew apart." Val sighed. "She wants to move to Europe and live there. I just want to stick to LA. I'm content managing my little store. She wants to travel the world while at the same time climbing the corporate ladder. That's just not for me, and my life just wasn't for her anymore."

"I guess that happens a lot, probably. How long were you two together?"

"Since I was twenty-five. So, nine years."

"I've never been with anyone for longer than a year. That's a long run," Avery said.

"It was. I feel like I'm at that age, though, where I don't know where to go to meet new people. My work consists of five employees who are all working their way through college; and I wouldn't date someone who worked for me anyway. Outside of that, I have my friends that I've had since forever. Most of them are married with kids, or at least in long-term relationships. Then, there's me with my busted up one." Val sighed. "I came to this party tonight hoping I'd maybe find someone to go on a date with me. Looks like I homed in on one that's already taken, though." She lifted herself up off the wall.

"There's still time. I'm sure this party will go on well past midnight."

"I don't know how late I'm going to stay up myself, though." The woman turned her head to look down the hall. "Waiting on your girl?"

"I don't know that she's *my* girl, but yeah. She should have been back by now."

"Maybe someone else is talking her up like I was doing with you," Val suggested.

"Maybe," Avery said. "She shouldn't be taking this long. Last time she did, another woman tried to pick her up. I should go find her, right?"

"And claim her like she did to you at the pool?" Val smirked at her.

"Yes," Avery stated firmly.

CHAPTER 17

"HEY, Mad. What's up?" Lennox asked. "Whoa there. Did you just down that whole thing?"

Maddox had indeed just downed an entire rum and Coke in one giant gulp.

"I did, yes." She put the now empty glass, save the ice that hadn't had a chance to melt, back on the bar and walked toward the back door of the house.

"What's going on?" Lennox asked, her tone turning concerned.

"Nothing. Is it midnight yet?"

"Almost. Like, five minutes. Why? Where's Avery?" Lennox followed her outside. "Also, where's my wife? I need to kiss her soon."

"I don't know where Kenzie is, but Avery is upstairs, talking to some woman who was obviously hitting on her earlier and is now hitting on her again."

"Hey, wait." Lennox pulled back on her arm once Maddox's feet hit the sand. "What? I thought you two were in Sienna's room. That's what Peyton told me."

"We were. We were talking. It was going well. Then, we left, and now, she's talking to someone else."

"Okay." Lennox lifted Maddox's chin so that she could meet her eyes. "Do you like this girl, Mad?"

"Yes, Lennox. Why do you think I just drank an entire rum and Coke in one gulp?"

"Why aren't you up there fighting for her, then?" Lennox asked. "God, when I thought I'd lost Kenz, I lost myself there for a while. Remember, that damn summer camp?"

"Yes, I remember you two being all over each other," Maddox replied.

"And then, she freaked out because she thought I was taking a job that would keep us apart. We worked through that. Then, more crap got thrown at us, and we got pulled apart for real. I had to fight for her, Mad. I had to make her see that she was the one for me. I didn't give up. Neither should you. So what if Avery is talking to someone else? Who's to say anything is happening between them? Who's to say she's actually interested? What if she's just talking to her because you're not there?"

"All good questions," Maddox said.

"Don't you want to find out the answers?"

"Yes," Maddox said, grunting a little.

"Why are you down here, then?"

"I went through so much with Jess, Len."

"Oh," Lennox said.

"I'm not saying Avery is like Jess or is Jess or…" She looked down at the ground and kicked off her shoes. "Just seeing someone I like talking to another woman who's clearly interested in more than just talking is still kind of a lot for me."

"What did you see?"

"Nothing, really. I had to go downstairs to use the bathroom because the other one was occupied, and when I walked back up, she was standing in the third-floor hallway with the woman from the pool, and they were smiling and laughing."

"What were they talking about?"

"I don't know. I couldn't hear. The music was too loud."

"So, you're freaking out… because?"

"Because I'm me." Maddox looked over at the dying bonfire. "I know. It's not fair to her."

"No, it's not."

"I'm over Jessica, I swear."

"You can be over someone and still have baggage because of the things they did to you. Jess cheated on you repeatedly and knowingly. Then, she tried to blame you. You took her back – for some unknown reason – and then she kissed someone else and still tried to blame you. I have no idea who Avery is or if that's something she's done before or would ever do to a girlfriend, but she doesn't deserve to be blamed for Jessica's bad behavior."

"I know. You're right. She told me she wants to see where this goes with us."

"Why are you down here talking to me, then?" Lennox asked.

"I felt like I needed a drink. I have no right to walk up and interrupt whatever was going on with them. I've already done that once, but I almost walked right up to them and took Avery's hand and pulled her into Sienna's room. That sounds terrible, doesn't it?"

"Depends on what you were planning on doing with her when you got there."

"Probably back her up against the wall and finally do what I've been thinking about doing all night."

"Okay. I get the picture." Lennox laughed. "You're totally into this woman. It's nice, Mad. I haven't seen you like this in a long time. Don't let whatever Jessica did, get in the way of this."

"Hey, guys," Peyton said, running up to them from the beach. "So, Dani had this idea that is totally crazy, but I'm going to do it."

"Have another kid immediately after you have the first one?" Lennox asked.

"You're that kid's Godmother, Lennox, so you better shut your mouth," Peyton said playfully. "When midnight hits, we're running into the water."

"You're what?" Maddox asked.

"It'll be fun."

"It'll be cold. It's one thing to put your feet in it.

You're going to run into the ocean in December?" Maddox asked.

"No, we're going to run into the ocean in January, Mad. It will be after midnight."

"Fair enough," Maddox said.

"Anyway, we're all going to do it. Well, not all of us, but a lot of us."

"Where's Kenz?" Lennox asked as she looked around.

"Over by the water. She wants to do it, too."

"No, she doesn't," Lennox said. "My wife? Kenzie? Kenzie Smyth? Adorable and sexy creature? She told you she wants to run into the ocean in the middle of the night?"

"She did. She's full of surprises now that she's all married to you, Lex," Peyton said.

"I guess so." Lennox smiled. "Years and years with someone, and they still surprise you. That's pretty cool, isn't it?"

"I wouldn't know," Maddox replied.

"No downers right now, Mad. We're going to celebrate the new year. Where's Avery?" Peyton looked toward the house.

"Upstairs."

"In Sienna's room?"

"No, I locked it. I have the key." Maddox pulled it out of her pocket and passed it to Peyton. "She's talking to someone."

"Oh, are you not going to find her in the next, like, two minutes?" Peyton asked.

"She should," Lennox added. "You should find her and talk to her, Maddox."

"She should find her and kiss her, Len." Peyton shoved Maddox's shoulder playfully. "You do want to kiss her, don't you?"

"Definitely," Maddox replied.

"Well, go find her."

Maddox looked toward the water and the people who were gathering near its edge. Some of them were dipping their toes in cautiously and running back into the sand from the cold. Others were kicking off their shoes. Some were taking off their shirts. Others were taking off pants, planning to go in there in only their underwear. For some reason, Maddox really wanted to join them. She didn't know why, but the thought of jumping into freezing cold water at midnight at the beginning of a brand-new year felt like a perfect way to start over, to get a fresh start, and to put every problem her relationship with Jessica had caused behind her.

"I'm going in," she said.

"To the ocean?" Lennox asked.

"Yes. You should, too."

"I will if Kenzie is," Lennox said. "Speaking of which, I'm going to go find my surprising wife."

"Hey, what happened with Avery?" Peyton asked her.

"Nothing. I'm just being really stupid."

"You usually are," Peyton said, lifting an eyebrow at her.

"I'd never had anyone cheat on me before; at least, not that I know of. Jessica really threw me. Then, she was here tonight, and with Lisa, no less. I can't believe they walked in on Avery and me and were about to do it on your bed."

"Yeah, me neither. Remind me to make sure everyone knows they're not invited to my house ever again."

Maddox heard someone yell that there was less than one minute until midnight.

"Where's Dani?" Maddox asked.

"By the water, waiting for me. We're running in together."

"Then, let's go do this."

"What about Avery?"

"It's just a midnight kiss. It won't be the end of the world if we miss it, and that's assuming she'd even want that." Maddox looked at her friends, who were ready to run into freezing cold water. "I wouldn't make it to her in time anyway," she said. "Let's go."

CHAPTER 18

"WHERE the hell is she?" Avery asked Val as they made their way down the stairs.

"I don't know. There are a bunch of people outside."

Avery heard someone say that there were only thirty seconds to midnight. Her heart began racing inside her chest.

"I thought she was coming back up," Avery said.

"Go find her. Get that midnight kiss, girl." Val shoved her toward the back of the house the moment their feet hit the floor.

"Thanks. Happy New Year!" Avery half yelled as she moved quickly through the crowd of people standing around the big-screen TV in the living room.

"Hey, Avery," someone she'd met earlier but couldn't remember her name, yelled at her as she exited the house.

She waved in their direction as her eyes scanned the patio, pool area, hot tub, and the beach. Where the hell was Maddox? Had she just left? No, she wouldn't have done that without talking to Avery. They were supposed to meet back at Sienna's room. Avery had been looking forward to sharing the rest of the night with Maddox in there, away from everyone else. With her head on a swivel, she finally found Dani and Peyton over by the water's edge. Figuring her best shot to find Maddox was to find Maddox's friends, she headed in that direction, kicking off her shoes as she went and not even paying attention to where they ended up.

"Ten!"

"Nine!"

"Eight!"

"Seven!"

Avery made her way past the bonfire.

"Six!"

"Five!" people continued to yell the countdown.

Avery spotted Dani and Peyton holding hands and leaning toward the water. Then, she noticed Kenzie and Lennox beside them, doing the same thing. Finally, she saw Maddox on their other side.

"Four!"

"Three!"

"Two!"

She rushed in Maddox's direction just in time for the crowd to yell, "One!"

Then, everyone at the water's edge rushed toward the ocean. Avery stopped for a second, hearing people scream and yell. Some of them yelled actual words, and the others just yelled nonsense. Maddox was among the latter group as she ran into the waves, letting them crash around her fully clothed body. Avery watched the woman disappear into the waves and pop back up after, running her hands through her hair. Then, Avery was running into the water, too. She hadn't thought about it. She'd just started running. She did remember to toss her phone onto a random blanket. She heard a lot of 'Happy New Year' messages as the water hit her feet, and then her knees, and finally, her waist.

"Maddox!" she yelled.

Maddox turned her head to Avery. They were a few feet apart now. Maddox moved toward her. Avery did the same. When they met, Avery didn't just kiss Maddox. She didn't peck her lips. She didn't give her a simple cheek kiss that friends exchanged. She took Maddox's face in both hands, pulled Maddox toward her, and kissed her hard. Their lips were salty from the water and needy for each other. Maddox's arms went around Avery's waist, and she pulled Avery into her body. Avery lifted herself up and wrapped her legs around Maddox as her own tongue moved into Maddox's mouth.

She didn't care that her dress and sweater were probably ruined. She didn't care that she was making out with Maddox in front of a crowd or that she was freezing cold. She only cared that she was kissing Maddox Delaney. Maddox's tongue slid against her own, causing Avery to groan into the woman's mouth. Her center was pressed against Maddox's stomach. Her legs tightened around her back. She felt her own hips move into Maddox. Then, she pulled back a little.

"Why'd you stop?" Maddox asked, looking a little stunned.

"Because I just…" Avery couldn't finish. "I mean, I could feel my…"

Maddox looked down and said, "Oh." She looked back up at Avery and smiled at her. "I didn't mind."

"I should…" Avery climbed off Maddox.

"What brought that on?" she asked as she cupped Avery's cheek and reached for her waist with her other hand, pulling Avery back into her body.

"I thought you were coming back upstairs. I wanted a midnight kiss. When I saw you out here, I didn't really have a choice."

"And how was it?" Maddox's smile was adorable.

"I thought it was pretty good."

"Me too."

"And now that the heat from that kiss is gone, I am freezing. So, can we–"

"Oh, yeah."

They made their way through the waves to the shore along with the others who had taken the midnight dip. Avery was suddenly very, very cold. She wrapped her arms around her body and wished she had thought to bring a towel to the beach, but she hadn't exactly been planning on running into the ocean to start her new year. Maddox looked around and quickly moved to pick up one of the blankets from the pile. She walked briskly back over to Avery and wrapped it around her, stepping into it herself and letting Avery wrap her arms around her neck. Maddox's were around her back, rubbing up and down.

"Thank you," Avery said, resting her forehead against Maddox's shoulder.

"You're welcome," Maddox replied. "And Happy New Year," she whispered.

Avery lifted her head up to look into Maddox's eyes. Maddox leaned back in and pressed her lips to Avery's. Avery couldn't hear the laughing, the screaming, the comments about being cold, or the waves crashing. She could only hear Maddox's light moans and the woman's breathing as they kissed. Avery hadn't been kissed like this in a long time; maybe ever. Maddox's hands weren't directly on her skin, but she could swear she could feel them touching her.

"Happy New Year," Avery replied when they pulled apart.

"Well, *hello*," Peyton said. "And I have extra clothes inside for you two."

"So, that happened," Dani added.

Avery couldn't pull away from Maddox without taking the blanket they were sharing, and she wouldn't do that. She could feel Maddox shivering against her body.

"Babe, get inside that blanket. You're pregnant." Peyton reached over and tucked a blanket more securely around her wife.

"It's freezing," Kenzie exclaimed as she wrapped a blanket around Lennox and moved into her side so they could both benefit from its warmth. "Why did we do that?"

"I don't know. It was your idea," Lennox replied. "Peyton, we're borrowing clothes."

"Yes, Lennox. I'm aware. I'll go get some stuff. You can all figure out whatever you want to steal. Let's go inside."

The four of them rushed toward the house, laughing.

Kenzie chased Lennox, who had taken off with their shared blanket. Peyton made sure Dani was covered the whole time, and Avery thought there was something so sweet about their relationship. She had always thought it was real, but one never knew how good two people were together until they spent some time with them; and it was clear Dani and Peyton were perfect for one another. The way Lennox stopped running from Kenzie, turned around, wrapped her arms around her body, and pulled her in for a kiss as she made sure the blanket covered Kenzie's body, spoke to how perfect they were for one another, too.

"Let's go put on something dry," Maddox suggested.

"But as cold as I am, I'm actually really enjoying just standing here with you," she replied.

"Me too," Maddox said, smiling at her. "But I don't want us to start off our new year losing fingers or toes to frostbite." She chuckled at her own joke.

"Fine." Avery frowned playfully.

"You're cute when you pout," Maddox said, leaning back in.

"I'm not pouting," she argued.

"Yes, you are." Maddox pressed her lips gently to Avery's.

"Well, I'm not anymore," Avery said.

Maddox's smile was contagious. She pulled on Avery's hand, and they made their way toward the house, sharing the blanket with Avery and picking up her phone on the way. They dropped the blanket on the patio before they went inside. They didn't say anything to one another as they quickly made their way up to Peyton and Dani's bedroom, where they saw Lennox and Kenzie rifling through clothes Peyton was tossing onto the bed.

"Dani has all these free underwear. So, take your pick," she explained.

"Free underwear?" Avery asked Maddox.

"She's a model. They get free stuff all the time. Come on." She pulled on Avery's hand.

They each settled on a shirt and a pair of pants. Avery wasn't going to change her underwear, but Maddox took a pair of brand new, still in the package, black ones, that looked like something Avery would enjoy taking off of her later. She cleared her throat at the thought.

"Avery, seriously, grab whatever you want," Dani said as she emerged from what must have been their bathroom. "Pey and I get so much free stuff, it's ridiculous. We have a whole closet of stuff. We give things away at least four times a year."

"Thanks." Avery grabbed a pair of underwear she wasn't sure would fit.

"Bathroom?" Maddox asked her. "You can go first."

"Sure. Thank you." She smiled at her thoughtfulness.

Avery walked down the hall at the same time Peyton and Dani disappeared into their master bathroom to finish getting changed and, probably, also make out if the eyes Peyton was giving Dani when she'd emerged the first time were any indication. Avery closed the guest bathroom door behind herself and locked it. She let out a deep breath, pulled off her sweater, and then unzipped her side zipper, sliding her dress off her body. She took off the panties she knew were ruined and left her bra on since she hadn't seen one of those on the bed. Her breasts were still swollen from arousal, but her nipples that had been peaked also due to arousal were now likely still only hard because of the freezing cold water she had just jumped into.

"What was I thinking?"

"Don't regret it," Maddox's voice came from the other side of the door.

"What?" Avery asked back.

"You just asked yourself what you were thinking. I'm just hoping you don't regret the kiss."

"No, Mad. I don't regret that," Avery replied, sliding the new underwear over her legs, feeling it a little tight around her thighs, but not having much of a choice. "I don't regret anything."

"Then, what did you mean?"

Avery slid the yoga pants over her legs and said, "Just that running into the water at midnight was crazy."

"That's all?" Maddox checked.

"Yes, that's all."

She pulled on a T-shirt that was a little too tight over her boobs. The water from the bra darkened the light-green shirt in some pretty specific spots. Avery washed her hands and splashed a little water over her face.

"*I* kissed you, Maddox," she added after a second.

"I know. But when I came back upstairs, you were talking to the pool girl."

Avery smiled as she wiped her hands and face and stared down at her clothes, wondering what to do with them. She picked everything up off the floor and opened the door to see Maddox standing there, holding a pile of clothes of her own.

"Get in here," Avery said, tugging on Maddox's arm.

"Hey," Maddox exclaimed through her laugher. "You're staying?" she asked when Avery closed the door behind them.

"I'll turn around," Avery replied. "And I know you know her name is not *pool girl*. Her name is Val. Well, it's Venice Valentine, but she goes by Val."

"Her name is Venice Valentine, and she's *not* a stripper?"

"Change your clothes, Maddox." She laughed. "And you don't need to be jealous. She just needed to go to the bathroom. I was only talking to her because I was killing time waiting for you. You took forever, by the way. Then, you didn't come back."

Avery watched as Maddox unbuttoned her shirt. Her eyes flitted up to Maddox's.

"You were supposed to turn around," Maddox said.

Avery then did just that, but she couldn't help but think about the sound of Maddox's buttons being undone. This woman was taking off her clothes right behind Avery in a somewhat cramped guest bathroom, and Avery was just standing there.

"I thought we talked about her before. I made it pretty clear that I wanted to get to know *you* more and that you didn't have to worry about her," Avery said.

"You did. I've just got some baggage I'm still dealing with, I guess."

"Like what?" Avery thought she knew the answer, but she also didn't want to assume.

"Just the regular old not trusting someone because someone else cheated on me, kind of baggage. It's the standard romantic comedy or soap opera type stuff." Maddox must have put the shirt and pants on because she said, "You can turn around now."

Avery did and said, "I'm sorry she treated you like crap, Maddox, but I wasn't going to do anything with Val."

"You can do whatever you want." Maddox shrugged. "You're not cheating. It just kind of hit me that it would bother me if you and Val *did* do something. It hit me before by the pool, but then especially after we talked in the loft and we got to know one another more and you had your hands on my legs. I don't know. It just hit me that it would really hurt to see you with someone else."

"I think that's a good thing, don't you?" Avery asked.

"I hope so. Of course, if you had actually done something with her or told me you were going to go out with her after tonight, it would still hurt."

"I'm not going out with her, Maddox." Avery put her hands on Maddox's hips. "I'd like to go out with you."

"Yeah?" Maddox asked, placing her hands on Avery's collarbones. "When?"

"Wait. Are you not wearing a bra?" Avery looked down at the two erect nipples peeking through Maddox's new navy-blue T-shirt.

"No, I took it off. It's soaking wet," Maddox replied. "I see you decided to keep yours on." She looked down at Avery's breasts. "That's a shame."

"Hey, are *both* of you in there?" Lennox's voice came from the other side of the door. "If you're doing something in there, can you just open the door a crack or something and pass me Kenzie's sweater? She'd left it in there before she had the great idea to go outside and give us both hypothermia."

CHAPTER 19

"So, that was interesting," Lennox told Maddox.

"Running into freezing cold water just because it's the new year?"

"No, you making out with Avery in said freezing cold water," Lennox replied.

"I think it's sweet," Kenzie added.

"I think *you're* sweet," Lennox said to her wife, kissing her neck.

"I thought that super cheesy lovey crap died when people got married," Maddox teased.

They were sitting out by the bonfire that was now back to full strength. The heat from the fire had started to dry their hair. Kenzie was sitting between Lennox's legs. Every so often, Maddox would see her close her eyes at Lennox's touch, seem to process something, and then open her eyes again with a smile. Dani was holding on to Peyton in the same way on Lennox and Kenzie's other side. They were both talking to another one of Peyton's friends, who was leaning down beside them.

"You'll find out one day, I guess." Lennox winked at her. "Maybe one day soon?"

"Stop it," Maddox said.

"Where *is* Avery?" Kenzie asked.

"Her brother was about to take off, so she went to say goodbye."

"And you're not worried about the pool girl finding her and trying to steal her again?" Lennox asked.

"No," Maddox answered. "I was being stupid before. I should have just walked up to them like an adult, said hello, and let what was going to happen, happen. I'm an idiot who has some work to do on her baggage, but that kiss pretty much told me what I need to know."

"And what's that?" Dani asked, turning to pay attention to their conversation now.

"That she likes me."

"Oh, honey, she more than likes you," Dani offered with a smile. "That girl thinks you're hot stuff."

"That's true. She pretty much mounted you in the ocean," Peyton added.

"She did *not* mount me." Maddox laughed.

"Her legs were all wrapped around you. Don't think we missed that part, Mad," Peyton argued.

"I saw it," Dani said.

"Me too," Kenzie added.

"Et tu, Brute?" Maddox joked.

"Don't throw your fancy college-educated references at us," Lennox said.

"Julius Caesar is, like, freshman year of high school, Len."

"Some of us went to school on studio lots, Maddox." Lennox glared at her playfully.

"Anyway, back to the part about Maddox getting humped in the ocean," Peyton said.

"Come on, Peyton. Don't be gross." Maddox picked up a small pile of sand and tossed it near Peyton and Dani, but not close enough to do any real damage.

"Was it gross? It looked pretty hot from where we were stalking; I mean, watching. No, I mean, not watching because that would be wrong," Peyton said with a smirk.

"Right." Maddox looked behind her, where she could see Avery talking to her brother and a few other people. "I'm going to ask her to come back to my place."

"You are, are you?" Dani said in a mocking tone.

"Yeah, I feel like I'd be crazy to just get her number

and wait a few days to call her so that I don't appear too eager. I *am* eager. I want to keep talking to her."

"Among other things," Kenzie said, to everyone's surprise, causing the entire group to laugh.

"Yes, among other things. She's a perfect kisser," Maddox said. "Not just amazing. She's perfect. It was a perfect kiss."

"We could tell. It lasted until the next new year," Peyton joked.

"It didn't last long enough," Maddox argued.

"Then, why are you still here, Mad? You've fulfilled your party obligation. You made it to midnight. You even jumped into the water with us. Go. Take your girl home," Peyton said, ushering for Maddox to go.

"You're assuming she'll say yes," Maddox returned.

"What kiss were *you* watching?" Lennox asked, chuckling. "She'll say yes."

"Hey," Avery said as she approached. "Can I sit?" she asked Maddox.

"Of course," Maddox replied, shifting over to give Avery some space on the blanket.

But Avery didn't sit next to her. She glanced at the couples sitting by the bonfire and knelt in front of Maddox, pressing her knees apart and then turning to sit between Maddox's legs. Maddox couldn't stop her smile. She knew it was embarrassingly wide and gave away how good this felt. When Avery leaned against her, Maddox wrapped an arm around the woman's waist and used her free hand to move Avery's hair away from her neck so that she could rest her chin there instead.

"Hi," Maddox whispered.

"Is this okay? I just kind of assumed." Avery turned her head a little to whisper back.

"Yes," Maddox answered a little too quickly.

"Okay. I just have to say it," Dani began.

"No, you really, really don't, Dani," Maddox argued.

"Yes, I do. You two are so cute," Dani said.

Maddox could feel Avery's laugh more than she could hear it over the sounds of the waves and the party around them. It was a pretty amazing feeling.

"Thank you?" Avery asked more than said.

"I'm sorry. My friends are idiots," Maddox offered her.

Avery wrapped her arms around Maddox's on her stomach and said, "I think they just care about you and like seeing you happy."

"It's been a while. I almost didn't know what that looked like, Mad," Peyton said, and Maddox knew she wasn't kidding.

"I've been going through some stuff, but I'm good," Maddox said, kissing Avery's shoulder through her shirt. "I'd be better if we started talking about something else; *anything* else, really. I'd settle for religion, politics, our opinions on how *Game of Thrones* ended…"

"Okay, but… Really? With that finale?" Peyton said.

And Maddox knew Peyton would be arguing with Lennox for the next twenty minutes at least about how they both wanted something different to happen in the end, and Lennox had been right. Maddox heard something about dragons from Dani's mouth before Peyton went on another rant.

"Hey, do you want to maybe get out of here?" Maddox asked Avery, running her fingertips against Avery's skin just above her hip. "And have I mentioned how I'm actually kind of glad you had to borrow a shirt? I can actually touch your skin now."

"You didn't seem to have a problem touching my skin when we were lying over there earlier," Avery countered. "And where do you want to go?"

"My place," Maddox suggested.

"Your place, huh?"

"She's the mother of dragons, Lennox," Peyton said rather loudly.

"Okay, but you get that she didn't actually birth them, right? It was some magic thing," Lennox replied.

"I think I'm going to go grab a drink or something. Want one, babe?" Kenzie asked, sitting up.

"Are you okay?" Lennox asked her, immediately dropping the argument with Peyton.

"Just tired. I was thinking about maybe taking a break."

"Want company?" Lennox asked her.

"No, I'm okay. Keep arguing with Peyton," the woman replied, kissing Lennox and then standing.

"Is she okay?" Avery whispered to Maddox.

"She's good," Maddox said. "They'll be talking about *Game of Thrones* for the next half hour, at least. It's been off the air for a while now, but Lennox only just binged-watched the whole thing for the first time, and they've been arguing about it ever since she finished. Kenzie's probably just exhausted from having to listen to it."

"She's right," Kenzie said as she walked past them. "Drinks?"

"I'm okay." Maddox looked at Avery.

"Not if we're leaving."

"*Are* we leaving?" Maddox asked.

"I'd like to," Avery replied.

"Guys, we're leaving," Maddox stated loudly, earning a smile and a silent laugh from Avery. "Happy New Year!"

Avery laughed as Maddox stood abruptly, forcing her to fall back on the blanket, making her laugh even louder.

"Nice, Mad. First, you win the girl. Now, you drop her on the sand?" Peyton said with a roll of her eyes.

"I'm fine. I'm fine." Avery sat back up.

"Sorry. I just got excited," Maddox said.

"Good thing she's not a guy, then," Lennox replied.

"Lennox!" Maddox reached for both of Avery's hands and pulled her up to a standing position.

"It's okay. I *am* glad you're not a guy, so it works out." Avery smiled at Maddox. "Let's go?"

"Yeah," Maddox replied. "Thanks for the party, Peyton," Maddox said to her friend.

"I can't wait to be thanked in your wedding toast. That's two for two, Dani. You owe me a—"

"Dinner." Dani promptly clapped her hand over Peyton's mouth, and her eyes went wide. "I owe her dinner. That's all. Only a dinner."

"Sure. Dinner and dessert after the sex," Lennox added as she stood. "And, Pey, you did not hook these two up. You can't claim that in the same way you can claim me and Kenz. You didn't even know Avery."

"No, but they met at our party," Peyton replied.

"That doesn't count," Lennox said.

"Why not?" Peyton asked.

"Okay. We're leaving," Maddox interrupted the friends, taking Avery's hand. "And if there's ever a wedding toast, we'll make sure not to ask any of you to do it."

"Boo!" Peyton laughed.

"Good night, guys. Thank you for coming," Dani said, standing to hug Maddox.

"Congratulations, Dani. I can't wait to meet the new little one," Maddox told her as she pulled away.

"Neither can I. Next week, want to get together to take some pictures?"

"Sure. Text me."

"I will," Dani said. "And have fun, okay?"

"Yes, Dani." Maddox laughed.

"I'm going to find Kenzie. I think she's probably about ready to go, too." Lennox looked around the beach.

"Peyton?" Maddox asked as she pulled Peyton in for a long hug. "Thank you," she said.

"I really didn't do anything; but I'm happy if you're happy, Mad."

"I am, I think," Maddox said as she pulled back. "And congrats to you, too. Since Lennox and Kenzie are joint godparents to Sienna, maybe I'll get to be a godmother for the new one?"

"Well, Dani and I are pretty traditional. We prefer our godparents to be married or, at least, settled down in a serious, committed relationship with someone we approve of, so I guess that depends on you, Mad." Peyton winked at her.

"I'm out of here before you just ask to perform the ceremony," Maddox joked.

"You ready?" Avery asked after she hugged Lennox.

"Let's get out of here."

CHAPTER 20

"SHOULD I change back into my dress and get these back to Peyton before we go?" Avery asked as they made their way through the house. "It's probably dry enough now."

"No, you can keep those. Trust me, they're not hurting for clothes."

"It feels weird wearing someone else's underwear, though," she said.

Maddox's hand tugged lightly on her own as Maddox stopped walking and looked Avery up and down.

"Now, all I can think about is you wearing sexy underwear."

"How do you know it's sexy?" Avery asked.

"I don't, but I want to," Maddox said.

Avery smiled at her, leaned in, and said, "Maybe you'll get to find out."

Maddox nodded and said, "Yes, please." Then she swallowed hard enough for Avery to see her neck muscles move with the motion.

Avery hadn't ever felt this wanted or desired in her life. Maddox had a way of looking both incredibly sexy and somewhat shy and surprised that Avery would want to be with her, which was endearing and only made Avery want her more. They made their way out to their cars after retrieving all their belongings from the house. They'd stopped only for a few minutes to look out over the beach from the balcony where they had a moment alone. Maddox had been behind Avery, running her hand up and down Avery's back before she moved into Avery and wrapped her arms around her. Avery could smell the salt on Maddox's hair and skin and thought about licking it off at the same time Maddox's palm rested on her abdomen just below her breasts.

The drive to Maddox's place in their separate cars seemed to take forever and no time at all at the same time. Avery was nervous. She wasn't someone who had one-night stands. She didn't just hook up with women after meeting them at a bar or a party. When she parked next to Maddox's car and glanced over at Maddox, who glanced at her and smiled, she had no idea what she was going to do if things escalated beyond the talking and now kissing that they had shared.

"So, this is my place," Maddox said as she let Avery walk in past her first.

"It's nice," Avery replied, looking around at the living room and kitchen area.

"I wasn't exactly expecting company, so it's not–"

"Maddox, it's fine. It's not like I was expecting to go home with someone tonight. Had you come to my place, it would have been pretty messy, too," Avery lied.

Her place was pretty spotless, usually. Whenever she found herself getting stuck on something in the code or in the science, she would stop and clean. Cleaning allowed the executive functions of her brain to turn off and the free, more creative part of her brain to take over. She would get herself back on track and would return to work for a breakthrough.

Maddox's place wasn't a disaster, but she didn't seem to have the same technique of using cleaning to be creative. Her coffee table had an empty paper plate next to a half-empty water glass resting on the dark wood. Her sofa had a jacket hanging over one arm and a few pillows out of place. The hardwood floor had a very nice rug over it where Avery could see one rogue shoe close to the table. She wondered for a moment where the other shoe was but looked away to take in the rest of the room.

"It's a two-bedroom, but the other one is my office," Maddox said. "And my sometimes dark room if I go old-school. The walk-in closet is surprisingly large enough and dark enough," she added.

"Is it good to have those chemicals in there?" Avery asked, concerned.

"I ventilate," Maddox replied with a smile. "So... I don't have any rum *or* any Coke, so I can't make you a rum *and* Coke, but I have several bottles of gift wine and probably a few beers. I haven't gone shopping since I got back from my trip."

"What is gift wine?" Avery asked, following Maddox into her tunnel kitchen.

"You know, when people don't know what else to give someone, they give them a bottle of wine? It's a pretty common gift for people when they're happy with the pictures I've taken. I get at least one a month, and I'm not a big fan of wine, so I mostly just take it with me to dinner parties and give it to other people."

"Not a big fan, or don't like it at all?" Avery asked, leaning against the counter.

"I'll drink it. If I have a choice, though, I'd have a beer or a rum and Coke, which is kind of how we met, isn't it?"

"Oh, God. Please don't tell my parents we met over a rum and Coke." Avery laughed a little.

"Why not?" Maddox asked, reaching into her wine rack for a bottle.

"They're snobby alcohol people. You know, the people that know the exact grapes used in the wine and can tell you that it has elements of oak or orange or cherry? They're like that. Plus, they're big bourbon drinkers. They have the whole setup at home and have one a night by their fireplace, which they have no reason to turn on because they live in Los Angeles."

"So, you don't want this probably twenty-dollar Merlot

I think I got from someone a few years ago when I did them a favor and took their engagement photos?" Maddox held it up.

"I'd rather have some coffee if you have it. It's late, and I'm tired, but I don't want to go to sleep yet," Avery said and then promptly blushed. "I just meant that I don't want to stop talking to you, and wine will put me to sleep."

"Are you sleeping over?" Maddox asked.

"Can I?"

Maddox put the bottle back and moved to stand in front of Avery. She leaned in, and Avery waited for her lips to touch her own, but Maddox just reached for the cabinet behind Avery and pulled out a container of coffee.

"Yes," she finally answered, meeting Avery's eyes with her sexy blue ones.

"Then, yes," Avery replied.

Maddox made the coffee as Avery stood there and waited. Every so often, Maddox would need to move around her, and she'd brush her hand over some part of Avery's body. When she reached for the sugar that was on Avery's right side, Maddox's hand brushed Avery's stomach over her shirt. When she pulled out the dry creamer, which was all Maddox had from a cabinet, and put it next to Avery, she reached for and squeezed Avery's hand. After she put two cups side by side, she leaned over and kissed Avery's neck.

"You smell like saltwater," Maddox muttered against her skin. "You taste like it, too." She kissed Avery's neck.

Avery gasped at the contact and said, "So do you." She wrapped her arms around Maddox's neck and held her in place. "It's good. I like it."

"Me too," Maddox replied before her tongue slid up the side of Avery's neck, and she sucked Avery's earlobe into her mouth. "Do you want to take a shower with me?" she whispered into Avery's ear.

"Yes," Avery whispered back, grasping the back of Maddox's shirt and pulling it hard, bringing her ever closer.

"Coffee can wait?" Maddox asked, kissing Avery's jawline.

"I don't think I'll need caffeine to keep me awake anymore."

Maddox kissed her then. Their tongues met, swirling around one another. Maddox started walking backward, likely toward her bathroom. Avery went with her, keeping their lips and bodies pressed together as close as possible. Maddox reached for the hem of Avery's borrowed shirt and lifted it up, forcing them to disconnect for a moment as she tossed it and reconnected their lips. Avery pulled Maddox's shirt off just as they made it to the hallway. They stopped for a second as Avery looked down at Maddox's full breasts. They were heaving. The nipples were hard and rosy. Avery wanted them in her mouth one at a time so that she could lavish them with the attention they deserved. Maddox's hands slid into Avery's pants and tugged them down.

"Nice," she said as she kissed the inside of Avery's thighs on the way back up her body. "Can I take them off?"

"Yes," Avery whispered as her heart raced inside her chest.

Maddox lowered herself again and kissed the waistband before she lowered the underwear to the floor, and Avery kicked them off. Maddox stared at Avery's patch of hair. As she licked her lips, Avery pressed her hands to the walls beside her, flattening her palms against both sides, expecting Maddox to take her right there in the hallway. Maddox stood, though, and kissed Avery as she kicked off and removed her own pants. By the time they were both nude, Maddox had the water going in her standing-only shower. Maddox walked in first, allowing Avery to watch the soft spray of the water roll down her skin. When Maddox opened her eyes and stared at her as the water fell over her face, Avery knew she wanted everything with Maddox Delaney. It had never hit her so quickly or so clearly in her life.

"Are you okay?" Maddox asked.

"Yes," Avery replied, moving into the shower and kissing her.

"As much as I want you in this shower, I also don't know that our first time should be—"

"Maddox, shut up," Avery said, pulling back to smile at her.

Maddox ran her hands up and down Avery's arms. Then, she reached around her for a loofa and a bottle of shower gel. Avery let Maddox run the lather over her skin as she watched Maddox take in her body. When Maddox's hand slid between her legs, Avery stood still against the wall.

"Do you want to take over?" Maddox asked her, kissing the now clean skin of Avery's neck.

"No, I've been taking over for myself for a long time. I'm ready for someone else to—" Avery blushed. "Oh, my God. I just admitted that."

"That it's been a while?" Maddox asked, sliding her head away.

"Yes."

"Well, would it make you feel any better if I told you it's been a while for me, too, and I needed it so much, I got myself off before I left for that party?"

"You did?" Avery asked.

"Yes." Maddox kissed her. "Had I known we'd be doing this, I definitely would have waited."

"When I left the party before, I went back to my place, sat on my sofa, and couldn't stop thinking about you." She slid her thigh between Maddox's. "I wanted you then, and I want you now," she added.

"Did you touch yourself?" Maddox asked between two shallow breaths.

Avery pulled her in closer, moved her mouth to Maddox's ear, and said, "I slid my fingers over my clit, but only on top of my underwear."

"Fuck. Really?" Maddox asked as Avery pressed her thigh to her sex. "God, Avery. I need to come." Maddox's hands gripped Avery's ass.

"You came today already. I didn't."

"It was yesterday, technically, and that was before," Maddox said, encouraging Avery's thigh harder into her sex as she rocked her hips against it.

"Let me wash you," Avery requested.

"After," Maddox said. "I'm close."

Her breathing was so ragged, Avery believed her. She didn't want to pull away, but she knew she wanted to touch Maddox for the first time when they were lying in her bed, not in the shower. Shower sex would come later.

"Babe, please," Avery said, removing her thigh. "Let me take care of you in here, and then I'll take care of you out there."

Maddox's eyes were dark with lust. The sound of the water falling down around them mixed with the sound of their heavy breathing.

"Whatever you want, Avery. I'll give you whatever you want," Maddox said.

CHAPTER 21

MADDOX had been so close to coming in the shower, her clit ached to finish. She swore under her breath as she wrapped a towel around her body to dry off.

"What's wrong?" Avery asked.

"Nothing," Maddox replied, tossing the now used towel to the floor.

"Really? Because I'm going crazy," Avery said.

"You are?"

"Take me to bed, Maddox," Avery replied, running her fingers between Maddox's breasts down to her belly button and then a few inches lower.

"You are killing me right now," Maddox said through gritted teeth.

"I've never done this before," Avery told her.

"Done *what* before?" Maddox asked.

"Just met someone and gone home with them," she said.

Maddox took Avery's hands and held them in her own.

"We can slow down," Maddox told her. "I mean, I'm about to come apart from touching you, and I haven't even really touched you yet, but we can slow down."

"I do like slow," Avery said.

Maddox let out a deep breath, trying to cool off her blood, and said, "Then, I'll grab you something to wear, and I–"

Avery kissed her and pulled Maddox into her bedroom. Avery's hands moved to her back and then her ass before they slid back up around Maddox's neck and started playing with the ends of her wet hair.

"I didn't mean I wanted to slow down like that. I just meant that I like slow. I like taking my time."

"Oh," Maddox said.

"But, I love how noble you're being right now." Avery smiled at her.

"Really? It's not making this whole thing less sexy?"

"No, but I'm pretty sure if we wanted to make it sexier, we can get there pretty quickly," Avery told her.

"Yes, I agree." Maddox nodded, earning a soft laugh from Avery. "Lie down, Avery."

Avery turned her head around, giving Maddox the best view of her long neck, and asked, "Is that where you..." Avery turned back to her. "Earlier, is that where you touched yourself?"

"Yes," Maddox confirmed, feeling the heat on her cheeks.

"What did you do?"

"You were right about making things sexier quickly," Maddox said. "I have a vibrator."

"Where is it?" Avery asked.

"Drawer." Maddox pointed.

"I'm not usually a vibrator girl myself. I have one, obviously; I just prefer my own hand most of the time." Avery sat on the side of the bed and opened the drawer, where Maddox kept her socks and her sex toys. "You have a few, it seems."

"When you order one online, they always give you a free one," Maddox said in defense. Then, Avery looked up at her with a smirk and the sexiest eyes Maddox had ever seen. "I used the black one."

"This one?" Avery pointed.

"Yes."

"Not this one?" Avery pointed at the flesh-tone dildo next to a blue rabbit-style vibrator.

"No," Maddox said.

"Do you like it when you do?"

"Yes."

"Do you have–"

"Shorts are under," Maddox finished for her. Avery opened the second drawer where she kept her underwear and a certain pair of shorts she'd bought with the dildo. "I've never actually worn them."

"Why not?" Avery asked, removing them from the drawer and placing them on the bed.

"I got them a few months ago. I had this idea that I needed to sow my wild oats or something and sleep with a bunch of women." Avery lifted an eyebrow at her. "I didn't. I realized that wasn't me, but I already had all the... stuff." Maddox nodded toward the drawer.

"Do you want to use any of this tonight?"

"Yes," Maddox answered honestly and instantly, earning herself another look from Avery. "Whatever you're comfortable with."

"What's this one feel like?" Avery asked, picking up the black vibrator.

There Maddox was, standing up next to her own bed, completely and totally naked, talking to a woman about her sex toy collection. Her nipples hardened as Avery brought the long, thin vibrator to her lips and sucked it into her mouth.

"Holy shit!" Maddox exclaimed. "Do that again, please."

Avery repeated the gesture, and Maddox about came from the sight of it.

"Like that?"

"Yes," Maddox answered in a whisper. "Can you turn it on?"

Avery twisted the bottom, and the sound of the vibrator filled the silent room.

"Now what?" Avery asked.

"Lie back," Maddox said.

Avery moved to lie against the pillows, still holding on

to the vibrator. Maddox crawled on top of her and took it from Avery's hand.

"I think we made it sexier again," Avery said, speaking Maddox's earlier thoughts into reality.

"I think so," Maddox replied.

"Are you going to show me how it feels now?"

"Yes," Maddox said.

Maddox sat up, straddling Avery. She took a moment to look at her and smile before she took the vibrator and touched it to Avery's neck, dragging it down her collarbone.

"That's not exactly what I had in mind," Avery told her.

"You wanted slow," Maddox reminded.

Maddox slid the vibrator to Avery's nipple, earning a gasp from her lover when she held it in place. She couldn't resist taking Avery's other nipple into her mouth.

"Can I take it back? Can I have it fast instead? I'd really like to have fast right now." Avery said as Maddox sucked her nipple into her mouth.

"No," Maddox said, kissing her way to Avery's other breast and placing the vibrator on Avery's now wet nipple.

"I'm not the one that got off earlier today, Maddox."

"It was twice," Maddox stated, playing with Avery's nipple with her teeth.

"Twice?" Avery's hips lifted and lowered.

"Once with this thing," Maddox said, lifting herself up to watch as she moved the vibrator over Avery's soft skin. "And once with my fingers."

"How did it feel?"

"Not nearly as good as it's going to feel when I make you come," Maddox said.

"Where were your fingers?"

Maddox placed the vibrator on Avery's thigh and squeezed her own legs together. Since she was straddling Avery, that meant Avery's thighs squeezed, too.

"Inside me," Maddox said as she rocked her center down into the vibrations she could feel.

"Don't stop," Avery said, grasping Maddox's ass. "Don't stop. Come for me."

"What does it feel like for you?"

"It's not where I need it," Avery said. "You did that on purpose."

Maddox leaned down and kissed Avery hard. The vibrations were faint. It probably needed a new battery already. It was old and always ran out quickly these days, but her clit could still feel it, and it was bringing her close to orgasm.

"I need to stop." Maddox sat up, still rocking her hips. Her hands went to Avery's breasts, and she squeezed them. "I can't. This feels so…"

Avery sat up, which dislodged the vibrator, but her lips were on Maddox's nipple. She sucked hard as she dipped her hands between her own legs and put the vibrator back where it was. Maddox rocked harder, and Avery sucked on Maddox's other nipple before she moved to Maddox's neck and sucked hard.

"I'm going to come, too," Avery said after a moment. Maddox stopped then, and Avery looked at her. "Why'd you stop? I'm so close, Maddox." She tried to use her hands to get Maddox to move her hips again.

"Because I'm making you come first."

Maddox reached between them and pulled out the vibrator. She tossed it aside and kissed Avery hard. She lay Avery back down and looked into her eyes.

"I can't believe I met you," Avery said, running her hands up and around Maddox's neck.

Maddox kissed her. She lowered her lips to Avery's neck, breathed her in, and nipped at her skin. She sucked on Avery's nipples again, one at a time. She lowered herself to Avery's stomach and kissed every spot before she swirled her tongue around her belly button. As she hovered over Avery's center, she used her fingers to stroke her thighs. Avery's chest was rising and falling rapidly. Maddox kissed the soft hair at the base of Avery's thighs. Then, she spread

Avery's legs wider and settled between them, kissing her.

"You can tell me to slow down," Maddox said, kissing her in the same spot again. "Or go faster now."

"Faster, Mad," Avery said, placing her hands on Maddox's shoulders and pressing down.

It was the first time Avery had called her Mad, which told Maddox she really did want her to go fast now. Maddox licked her once, earning a gasp and rising hips. She then licked her again, tasting Avery really for the first time as she swirled her tongue in her desire. Maddox opened her eyes when one of Avery's hands disappeared. She looked over to see it in a fist at Avery's side as Maddox sucked the woman into her mouth. Then, it moved to Avery's breast. Avery played with her own nipple as Maddox sucked her harder. Avery's clit was swollen and ready, and Maddox knew it wouldn't take long. She took one hand and covered Avery's other breast, squeezing it and tweaking the nipple. She used her other hand to move between Avery's legs. She then slid inside her with two fingers, not wanting to try with one first. She wanted her. She wanted all of her. Avery lifted up off the bed when Maddox curled inside her and flicked her clit back and forth with her tongue. She opened her eyes again to see that Avery was still twirling her nipple with her fingers. Maddox reached for the vibrator that they hadn't bothered to turn off – glad that the battery hadn't died yet – and placed it on Avery's nipple. Avery screamed words Maddox never thought she'd hear come out of this sexy little nerd's mouth. Maddox sucked again, wanting to make Avery come harder than she ever had before. When she began to thrust, Avery spread her legs wider, inviting Maddox in deeper.

Maddox slid the vibrator down Avery's middle and rested it just above Avery's clit. Avery moaned loudly then. Maddox lowered it until it could fit against her tongue and as she thrust inside hard and fast, Avery lifted her hips so high off the bed, Maddox had to hold her down; and she came. Maddox licked her and sucked as she continued to slowly move inside. Eventually, she removed the vibrator, still not caring to turn it off, and just continued to kiss Avery's clit. She wasn't done touching this woman, and she wasn't sure she ever would be.

"Amazing," Maddox said.

"That's my line," Avery breathed out.

CHAPTER 22

THAT WAS the sexiest sex Avery had ever experienced. She'd never had a woman use a vibrator on her like that, and despite how good Maddox's tongue and fingers felt, the vibrations added a whole other dimension, and Avery felt like jelly. She couldn't feel like jelly, though. She needed to touch Maddox. God, she wanted to touch every single part of that woman.

"Do you want something to drink now?"

Maddox had moved to lie beside her. Her fingertips were just grazing Avery's abdomen over and over.

"No," she replied, turning her head toward Maddox. "I want you."

Avery stood up and stared down at her.

"So, you're getting out of bed?" Maddox asked.

"I'm putting something on," Avery said.

She'd never done this before. Well, she'd been the receiver once, and it had felt nice, but she was also more than okay with a woman's fingers bringing her to orgasm. She was excited to do this with Maddox, though. She felt like a risk-taker tonight. She wanted to give herself to Maddox in all ways, and that included doing something she had never done before. She slid the shorts on her legs and looked down at the ring that now rested between her legs.

"You don't have to—"

"I want to," Avery interrupted. Maddox reached for the dildo, and Avery smiled as she handed it to her. "It's not very sexy, but can you maybe help me with—"

"Yes."

The soft hitch in Maddox's response made Avery think she did actually find this part sexy after all. Maddox sat on the side of the bed and helped get the dildo put in place.

Then, she just stared at Avery standing there. Avery felt like an idiot, but the way Maddox looked her up and down, had her feeling something quite different. She had only just had an earth-shattering orgasm, but Maddox's darkening eyes made her want to come again and again all night long.

"Lie back, Mad," Avery said, feeling better and more comfortable using the nickname she'd heard others use for Maddox all night.

She climbed on top of Maddox, and Maddox spread her legs immediately.

"You're beautiful," Maddox told her as she brushed her hair away from her face.

"I've never done this before," Avery said. "I mean, I understand how it works, obviously. I just might not be very good at it."

"Avery?"

"Yeah?"

"Just start by kissing me."

Maddox pulled Avery's face down to her own, and their lips met. Avery kissed her for long moments, reveling in the feel of their soft, warm lips dancing together. Then, she placed her lips on Maddox's neck and kissed down to her breasts. She had been wanting to touch them all night and didn't want to waste any more time. She sucked a nipple into her mouth and earned Maddox's hips lifting into her. Avery could feel the toy between her legs rubbing into her own sex, enough to make her clit throb harder.

"That feels good," she told Maddox.

"Yeah?"

"Yeah. I didn't think it would make me feel..."

"Hold on a second, okay?" Maddox requested.

Avery pulled up immediately and looked down at her, asking, "Is everything okay?"

"Yeah, I should have gotten it out sooner. I was a little distracted."

"Distracted?"

"Yeah, you're naked, Avery. I'm distracted." Maddox

reached for something inside the same drawer they'd pulled the other toys out of, and held it out in her palm. "This goes inside that little pocket in there." She wiggled her eyebrows toward the shorts. "It'll help." She met Avery's eyes. "If you're interested."

"I am," Avery said, taking the small vibrator and tucking it into the small pocket inside the shorts. Before she moved again, she pressed the button, turning it on and instantly feeling the vibrations pulse against her clit. "Oh, wow."

"I am so glad I bought this thing," Maddox said.

She reached up for her, kissing Avery again as Avery's hips started to rock on their own.

"I'm going to come soon if this thing stays on," Avery told her.

"Go inside me," Maddox said. "I need you inside. I have all night."

Avery grabbed the dildo in one hand and stared down at it, trying to figure out what to do next. She knew what to do; she just needed to do it. She placed a hand next to Maddox's head and moved the toy into Maddox's wetness, watching it as she slid it up and down, gathering Maddox's desire for her. Then, her eyes met Maddox's. Maddox's hands moved to her ass and slid under the shorts. She then lifted and lowered her eyebrows as if acknowledging that she wanted Avery inside now. Avery lowered the toy to Maddox's entrance and tentatively slid it inside.

"Like this?"

"Yes," Maddox said, rolling her head back and closing her eyes. "More."

Avery pushed it in more, and when it disappeared inside Maddox completely, she rested her now free hand on the other side of Maddox's head. She moved slowly at first, rocking into her. She leaned down and kissed Maddox as she pressed herself into her, feeling the vibrations begin to take over her own sensations. She tried to focus on the feeling of being inside Maddox like this; of being on top of her, kissing her, instead of the consistent pulsing between her own thighs.

"I like this," Avery said into Maddox's ear. "Do you?"

"Yes. God, I can feel the vibrator, too. Don't stop, okay?"

"I won't."

Avery rocked a little faster and then a little harder.

"Yes," Maddox said. "Just like that. Faster."

"I won't hurt you?" Avery asked and silently admonished herself.

"You won't hurt me. Just faster, baby. I want you."

Avery hadn't ever been called 'baby' before. It felt good. It felt really, really good in this moment as she rocked into Maddox. She lowered her head and sucked an erect nipple into her mouth. She moaned as she sucked on it, rolling her tongue around it. She moved harder and faster still. Maddox pushed her down farther, and they were rocking together. God, they were rocking together, and they were going to come together, and it was all too much and not enough at the same time.

"I'm coming," Avery told her.

"Do it," Maddox said. "Come again. God, I'm coming, too. Oh, yes!"

Avery's thrusts were a little more erratic, but she hoped they worked all the same because she couldn't control them. She was coming, and Maddox was coming with her. She kissed Maddox sloppily. Maddox tried to kiss her back as they both moaned and yelled out words to no one in particular. Avery's rocking slowed when Maddox's grip on her ass loosened and her hands more or less just stayed there.

"That was…" Avery started but couldn't finish the sentence as she flopped down onto Maddox's now clammy body.

"God!" Maddox ran a hand over her face. "I want it again."

Avery lifted herself up. Initially, she had planned to

turn the vibrator off, but she looked down at Maddox instead and waited for her to say something else.

"Again?" Avery asked when Maddox just stared up at her as she tried to catch her breath.

"Can I roll over?" Maddox asked.

"Yes," Avery replied, thinking Maddox Delaney was perfect for her.

Avery had always wanted a sex life like this with someone she cared about. She couldn't say *love* just yet. They had known one another less than twenty-four hours, and all the hormones from hot sex were likely clouding her brain, but she *was* crazy about Maddox. She knew that part already. She had dreamed of being on top of a woman, rocking into her as she came from her touch. She had made a woman come before, but her past lovers had always been so tentative, so basic, or vanilla, or whatever the term was that best fit the standard sex they'd shared. Avery liked standard sex just fine, but she'd be lying if she said there wasn't a part of her that wanted to flip Maddox over and take her from behind; to claim her as her own and make sure that Maddox knew she wanted her to only be touched by her. She wasn't quite that brave yet, though, so she let Maddox take a moment. Then, she slid out of her and waited for Maddox to roll over onto her stomach.

"Leave the vibrator on," Maddox requested.

"I was planning on it."

Avery grasped Maddox's hips first. She then lifted them up, liking the look of Maddox's ass in the air like this, and leaned down, kissed it, nibbled on it, sucked on it, and then licked the spot again. Then, she reached for the dildo and moved it into position. With her other hand on Maddox's hip, she slid it back inside Maddox and pulled Maddox toward her.

"Oh, yes."

Avery grasped both of her hips and moved Maddox back and forth as she moved her own hips in time with her. The vibrator wasn't hitting the same spot as before, but it was close enough. Avery could feel herself growing wetter and knew these shorts would need to be washed. She didn't care about herself right now, though. She only wanted to make Maddox come.

"There?" she asked.

"Right there," Maddox said.

Avery watched as Maddox reached a hand between her own legs and started rubbing her clit.

"Let me," Avery said.

She then reached around Maddox, and just as Maddox removed her own hand, Avery put hers in place and stroked Maddox's clit.

"Yes," Maddox said as she rocked forward and back. "Yes. There."

Avery stroked her slowly at first, wanting to work Maddox up a bit before letting her come again. Maddox seemed to be fine with that because she slowed her own movements and let Avery lead. That was sexy in and of itself. It meant Maddox already trusted Avery enough to let her touch her like this, to be this vulnerable with her. That was enough to make Avery want to go fast now.

"Will you come for me?"

"Yes," Maddox replied.

Avery pushed harder inside her. She stroked Maddox's clit with two fingers, pressing them hard against the woman. Maddox started to come, and Avery didn't want to stop. She stopped stroking her and put both hands on Maddox's hips, rocking harder and faster until Maddox came. Her face pressed into the pillow, and her cries of pleasure were muffled against it. Avery slowed but didn't stop entirely. She could feel her own orgasm building once more. She knew if she kept going, she'd come again.

"Wait," Maddox said, lifting herself up, and Avery stopped moving. "Take them off and get up here."

"What?" Avery asked.

"Lose the shorts. I want you," Maddox told her. "Sit on my face. Let me make you come."

Avery slowly pulled out and stood. She watched as Maddox rolled onto her back. Her skin was flushed and hot. She looked so sexy, Avery wanted to take her again, but she would give Maddox what she was asking for first. She turned off the small vibrator and lowered the shorts with the toy to the floor. Then, she climbed back on top of Maddox, straddling her waist.

"Did your clit come?" Avery asked her.

"Not yet, no. Come up here, though," Maddox said, reaching for her hips and trying to get her to slide up to her face. "I need to taste you again."

"Well, I need to taste you for the first time, so I don't know what to do about that." She smirked at Maddox.

"Oh, I think you do," Maddox replied, smirking back.

Avery turned around and moved her body until her throbbing sex was over Maddox's face, and her own mouth was hovering over Maddox's center.

"I'm already close. It won't take long," Avery said as she leaned down, moving her fingers to Maddox's folds to spread her first.

"Me too," Maddox said, and then she licked her.

Avery could barely keep herself up. Just that one touch had her nearly coming undone again. She remained focused, though. She moved her mouth to Maddox's sex and licked her, earning a few moans and vibrations against her own clit before she sucked Maddox fully into her mouth. A few minutes later, they were both panting their release and lying side by side on Maddox's bed.

"That was the best sex I've ever had," Avery stated the obvious.

"You said *that was* like it's over. I think you mean *this is* the best sex you're still having." Maddox climbed on top of her. "I'm nowhere near done with you yet, Avery Simpson."

CHAPTER 23

"THIS shower is somehow even better than the first," Avery said as Maddox stood up.

"Probably because this one included orgasms," Maddox replied, kissing Avery's neck.

"Multiple orgasms," Avery told her.

"Yeah? I didn't think I was down there *that* long," Maddox said as she sucked Avery's earlobe into her mouth.

Avery chuckled, and Maddox felt it against her skin, loving the sensation.

"You weren't. I just came that quickly," Avery confessed.

They hadn't stopped touching each other since they'd first started. The coffee had long ago been forgotten about. Their bodies were sore by now, and they should probably be sleeping, but they hadn't been able to stop. Maddox hadn't ever felt this before. Yes, she'd enjoyed sex with other women before. She'd argue she'd had pretty damn good sex before, but she and Avery had pretty *great* sex together. No, it wasn't just great. It was amazing. Maddox just couldn't think of another, less cliché word to use to describe it.

"Well, happy to help however I can," she told Avery.

"My legs are a little on the wobbly side, though. Any chance we could go back to bed now?" Avery asked, running her hands up and down Maddox's back.

"For sleep?"

"We probably should. When was the last time you slept, Mad?"

"Can I just tell you that I love how you say my name like that?" Maddox kissed her. "Everyone does it, but for some reason, when you do, it's hot."

Avery smiled at her and said, "Then, let's go lie back down, *Mad*." She emphasized the nickname.

"Actually, I'm starving." Maddox turned off the water. "Want to order something and eat it in bed?"

"Yes," Avery answered as she exited the shower, passing Maddox one towel and wrapping herself in another.

Maddox wrapped the towel around her own waist, preferring to let her breasts air-dry, and caught Avery looking at her.

"What?" she asked.

"We have got to put some clothes on you," Avery said, pointing at Maddox's chest.

"You've had your hands all over me for hours," Maddox replied.

"And I still would if I could actually feel my fingers."

"Well, they were inside me for about four orgasms, so I can understand why they'd be numb."

Maddox wrapped her arms around Avery's neck and pulled her in for another kiss.

"I have never had this much sex in such a short amount of time. I think my body might need a few hours to recover."

"Let's get some water in you, and I'll order us something to eat. Then, we can just lie around the rest of the day," Maddox suggested, walking around Avery to go find her phone.

Avery went to Maddox's kitchen and procured them two glasses of water, which they both promptly drank down. She refilled them and brought them back to the bedroom in time for Maddox to finish ordering them food. It was at that odd hour between breakfast and lunch, so their options had been fairly limited, but Maddox had managed – on New

Year's Day, no less – to get them diner food. With many of Maddox's exes, diner food had never been an option. In particular, with the few models she had dated, it hadn't even been allowed in the house. The mere smell of grease had been enough to make Jessica turn and run.

"I love greasy bacon," Avery told her as she leaned back against Maddox's pillows that she'd just had to put back in the right place. They had been strewn about the bed and floor for most of the night. "Especially, after drinking the night before."

"You are perfect," Maddox said, laughing and lying back next to her.

"You are naked." Avery lifted an eyebrow and gave her a once-over. "I thought you were going to put clothes on."

"You didn't put clothes on. And you just dropped your towel on the floor like you didn't think I'd have to climb on top of you and–"

"Okay. Okay. We need clothing," Avery interrupted through her own laughter.

"I'll get you something," Maddox said, standing.

"How is it I started the night in my own dress, but I have since worn borrowed clothing from Dani and Peyton and now you?"

"Does this mean you're wearing my underwear?" Maddox teased as she tossed a T-shirt and a pair of boxers onto the bed. "Or will that do for now?"

"This is good," Avery said, standing. "And you wear boxers?"

"Sometimes," Maddox replied. "I like to mix up my underwear. Sometimes, I'm in boxers. Other times, I'm in regular old bikinis." Maddox moved over to Avery as she slid an old shirt over her head. "Rarely, but it does happen, I'm in a thong."

She watched Avery gulp.

"You're evil, Mad," Avery told her and pulled on the shirt, bringing Maddox closer to her.

"I can put one on for you right now if you want,"

Maddox said, leaning into Avery further and leaving her lips millimeters away from Avery's.

"I'd only want to take it off you," Avery replied.

"That's not a problem, is it?" Maddox pressed her lips to Avery's briefly before pulling back and winking at her. "I'll put on my granny panties instead."

Avery laughed and said, "Compromise. Just put on a comfortable pair. You don't have to go full granny."

Maddox found a pair of boxers she liked and slid them over her bare legs. Then, she climbed back into bed with Avery.

"Ouch," she said, standing quickly and looking down to find whatever she'd just sat on. "Oh," she said when she found it and held it up for Avery to see.

"Your bed is littered with sex toys," Avery said, laughing.

Maddox tossed the vibrator into the drawer and moved to lie beside her.

"I think we used just about everything I own," Maddox told her, snuggling up to Avery's side.

"I'm so not used to being the big spoon," Avery said.

Maddox sat up and looked at her.

"Want to switch?"

"No." Avery smiled at her, rubbed her cheek with her thumb, and said, "It kind of feels right to me. I like holding you."

"And doing other things to me?" Maddox asked with a lifted eyebrow.

"Yes, I liked those things, too. Come here."

Maddox moved back into Avery's outstretched arms.

"I'm not used to being the little spoon if it makes you feel any better."

"So, do *you* need to switch?" Avery asked.

"No, I'm with you on this one. It feels really good, being held by you like this. It also felt good having you do all those things to me," Maddox replied and lifted herself enough to kiss Avery's neck.

"We should probably talk more, right?"

"Probably."

"So, I'm going to ask you out now, which I realize seems pretty ridiculous, given what we've been doing all night, but I think it's important," Avery said.

"I'm going to say yes, if that helps."

"I'm going to ask you *when* and hope that you say *as soon as possible.*"

"I'm going to say *as soon as possible*, so that works out well," Maddox said as she smiled at how silly they were being right after she'd had her mouth wrapped around Avery's clit in the shower.

"So, tonight?" Avery asked.

"Tonight, as in like, seven or so hours from now?"

"Too soon?"

"No, it's just kind of like one continuous date, though, isn't it? We met around six or so last night."

"So, what are we going to do for our twenty-four-hour anniversary?"

"Oh, please, do not tell me you're one of *those* women. First, it's the twenty-four-hour anniversary. Next thing I know, you want flowers *and* chocolates for the forty-eight-hour anniversary and a proposal on the seventy-two-hour one."

"No, I want the proposal on the forty-eight-hour anniversary, actually – with flowers *made of* chocolate," Avery corrected.

Maddox laughed hard at that and sat up. She then straddled Avery's hips and met her eyes.

"Fine, but we're getting married on day seven; no sooner. I've got a lot of planning to do in six days, and we still have to pick out cake flavors," she continued the joke.

"As long as the top layer can be red velvet, I can be okay with that." Avery kissed her.

"This is good, isn't it?" Maddox asked, kissing her back sweetly.

"We're crazy, but yes, this is good." Avery chuckled

against Maddox's chest as she pressed her face to it. "And I love your boobs. Have I told you that yet?"

"Yes, you've said it a few times," Maddox replied, running her hands through Avery's still wet from the shower hair.

"I've never really been a boob-girl, but I'm a boob-girl now," Avery said, lifting Maddox's shirt and looking at her chest directly. "Yeah, definitely a boob-girl now."

"I'm glad," Maddox said as Avery took a nipple into her mouth. "I thought we were taking a break."

"We were, but now your boobs are in front of my face. What am I supposed to do?"

The doorbell rang.

"Eat lunch with me," Maddox said, pulling back and smiling down at her.

"How'd it get here so fast?"

"It's just down the street," Maddox told her as she stood. "Stay here. I'll bring everything to you."

"Can you maybe start some more coffee? I think we're going to need it," Avery said. "I'm going to call Tony and make sure he got home okay, or at least check and make sure he's still alive. I should check a few work things, too."

"If you need to borrow a computer, you can grab my laptop. It's over there," Maddox told her, pointing to her dresser.

"I can do it all from my phone. Now, go get our food. I'm starving," Avery said, winking at her.

"For boobs, apparently," Maddox teased and left the room.

She made her way toward the front door and opened it, surprised when she didn't see the food delivery guy standing on the other side.

"Hey, Mad," Kenzie said softly.

"Kenzie? What are you—"

"I'm sorry to just show up like this. I should have called."

"No, it's okay. Come in," Maddox said, motioning her

inside. "Is Len parking the car or something?"

"No, it's just me." Kenzie shrugged as she turned around to face Maddox.

"Okay. Can I get you a drink? I was just about to make some coffee."

"Can I talk to you about something important?"

Maddox looked back toward the bedroom door, which she had left partially open, and said, "Sure. What's up?"

"I think I want to have a baby," she replied.

Maddox's eyes went wide.

CHAPTER 24

"HEY, I'm glad you're actually alive."

"Avery, who actually calls people these days? Just send a text," Tony replied with a groggy voice. "And it's not afternoon yet, so why are you calling me?"

"Because when we left it last night, you didn't know where you were going to end up since Dario seemed more interested in the other guy when you went behind those rocks to... talk."

"Yes, that's what we did. We talked. We talked about how my parts can fit inside–"

"Stop, Tony!" She closed her eyes, looked toward the partially open door, and lowered her voice. "I need some advice. That's really why I called."

"I assume you do not need advice about how gay men have sex?"

"No, I think I got the picture."

"And you're not about to talk to me about how lesbians have sex, are you?"

"Not specifically, no. Where are you?"

"I'm at Dario's."

"Really? You still went?"

"He more than made it up to me. Besides, he's very good."

"Well, I'm glad you had a good time, then," she said.

"Me too. Don't tell Mom or Dad or anything because I don't know what's going to happen, but I do actually like Dario. It's not just about sex."

"But you don't want Mom or Dad to know because you think they'll ask to meet him?"

"How exactly would you explain that you like a dancer who has a boyfriend that lives in another country and that you had sex multiple times with multiple partners and plan to do it all again when said boyfriend is in town to see if there's a good match between all three of you and if there is, you're considering being in a thruple?"

"And, in this scenario, Mom and Dad know what a thruple is?"

"You see my point," he replied.

"I do." Avery laughed. "And I won't say anything to them."

"Thanks. Anyway, what do you need advice about? Last I saw you, you were telling me about your new gal pals, Peyton and Dani."

"They're not my–" Avery paused. "Never mind." She took a deep breath and softly said, "I really like her, Tony."

"Dani? Or Peyton? Also, they're married… to each other."

"Maddox. Why would I like Dani or Peyton?"

"I don't know. I'm going off of hours of sex right now. I'm trying to keep up."

"Me too," Avery said before she could stop herself.

"Sorry, what?" he asked.

"Hours of sex with no sleep. I'm running on sex fumes." She squinted her eyes in embarrassment.

Tony burst out laughing and said, "No, Dario. I'm laughing at my sister. I'll be right there. Yes, put on another one. We're going again." Avery rolled her eyes. Then, his voice got louder. "You had sex all night?"

"Hours of it, yes."

"That good?"

"That perfect," she corrected.

"Women," he joked. "When are you moving in?"

"That's kind of what I wanted to talk to you about."

"Wait. What? I was kidding. You can't move in with her."

"I'm not." Avery laughed softly. "I'm just really into her, Tony. I want to do something nice for her. We're going on a real date tonight, and I have no moves."

"Not according to that perfect sex you had."

"Tony, I'm serious. You know I suck at dating."

"So, you want to what, take her somewhere nice?"

"Yes," she said. "But I don't know where."

"This is Los Angeles, Avery. Also, there's Google."

"Tony, please," she begged.

"I don't know. Take her to the beach."

"I'm sorry… Were we at the same party last night? We've already done the beach."

"A movie?"

"We sat in a movie theater. We didn't exactly watch a movie, but I don't think so."

"Take her to dinner in Santa Monica or something. There's a ton of cool places around there."

"So, your suggestion is dinner and a movie? I thought you were extra," she teased. "What good is it having a gay brother if he won't help me figure out—"

"I'm not your fairy godmother, little sister. Now, if you want, I can finish up with Dario later and meet you at your place to do your hair and makeup. I'll pick out your clothes for you, since I don't trust you to do it yourself and you're dating a woman who's been with supermodels, so I'll make sure you look good. You're in charge of the event planning, though."

She grunted and said, "Fine. I'll take what I can get. Can you be at my place at six?"

"What time are you meeting her? Nine?"

"No. I thought I'd pick her up at seven."

"Oh, honey, good work like mine takes time. I'll be

over there at four. Be showered, but don't dry your hair. I'll take care of that."

"Fine. I guess I'll start Googling."

"Have fun. I'm about to do some Googling myself," he joked.

"You're a terrible brother," she said, teasing him, and hung up the phone. Then, she looked at the door. "Where's the food?"

She used the time waiting for Maddox to scroll through her phone, but she was now pretty sure Maddox was watching TV or listening to something because she could hear the voices from down the hall. She assumed Maddox was taking food out of containers and maybe putting everything on plates. That seemed like something Maddox would do. The coffee had to be done by now, though, right? Avery looked up the top ten things to do in Los Angeles, feeling like a tourist and not someone looking to take her new *person* on a date.

What were they now? Were they dating? Were they together? Were they friends with benefits until they had the official conversation? She searched for top romantic spots in Los Angeles and found a couple that could work. She saved them in her phone and decided she needed to check on Maddox. She left the bedroom and made her way down the hall toward the kitchen.

"Mad, what's taking so long? I'm starving, and only a little bit of that is for you. Most of it is for actual food. Oh…" Avery stared straight down at Kenzie, who was sitting on Maddox's sofa next to Maddox herself.

"Hi, Avery," Maddox said, blushing and also smirking. "Kenzie stopped by."

"I'm sorry. I didn't know you had someone over, Mad. You should have told me." Kenzie stood.

"Kenz, it's fine." Maddox patted her leg. "Can you give us another minute, Ave?"

Avery tried not to smile at the nickname and said, "Of course. I'll just be back in the bedroom. I have some work to do anyway."

"It's okay. She can know," Kenzie said, looking down at the floor.

"Kenz, you don't have to tell anyone anything you're not ready for. Avery understands that."

"I think I want to have a baby. But I'm worried I told my wife no so many times, that if I tell her I want one now, *she's* going to say no, or ask me a bunch of questions I don't know the answer to. So, I came over here to talk to Maddox about it because I can't talk to Dani or Peyton. They're good friends, but Lennox can read both of them like books. She'll know we talked about something important. Maddox can keep it a secret."

"I'm a closed book," Maddox told her. "I'm basically one rung below secret agent." She winked at Avery. "Sit down?"

Avery sat next to her. Kenzie moved to the chair beside the sofa.

"So, you're ready for a baby?" Avery asked as Maddox slid a hand on her thigh like they did this all the time.

"I think so. I mean, is anyone ever really ready?"

"I have no idea," Avery said.

"Kenz, Lennox loves you. She won't care about the reasons if you're ready and you're honest with her."

"Can I ask why you said no before, or is that too personal?" Avery asked.

Kenzie looked at her and ran her hands up and down her jeans before she said, "I didn't want to pass down my Asperger's. I think my dad had it, too, which means it's pretty strong in the Smyth gene pool." She paused for a second. "Lennox used to say she'd have them, but she's older than me, and now, she's talking about how she's too old to have one herself."

"She told you that?" Maddox asked.

"I overheard her telling Peyton when they were talking about it," she replied.

"There's always adoption. Plenty of kids need homes,"

Avery suggested.

"You're right, and I know we'd both love to give a little one a home, but I've been starting to think about having a baby myself."

"That's great, Kenz."

"I just think I've worked really hard to be okay with myself, and if we do have a little one that is on the spectrum, I'd be able to help them in a way most people can't. Plus, Lennox's sister would be a great aunt if that's the case, too." Kenzie smiled so wide; Avery squeezed Maddox's hand.

"Len's going to love this idea, Kenz. She's always told me she'd be fine either way. She wanted you. She's always wanted you. And she's loved you for who you are and everything you bring into her life. This is just another thing you're bringing. She's going to love this."

"You don't think she's going to be upset that I've waited so long, and now she doesn't want to have the baby herself?"

"I don't think so, no." Maddox slid her fingers into Avery's. "It'll be your son or daughter. Besides, she's not *that* old. If she does want to have one, she can."

"I guess so," Kenzie said. She then bit her lower lip and added, "She's the love of my life." She shrugged a shoulder. "I didn't think I could do it until I saw Peyton and Dani with Sienna. They're amazing moms. And then I saw Lennox with the baby, and I just knew she'd be an amazing mom and that I wanted that for her."

"She'd be fine just being a cool aunt, you know that, right?" Maddox said.

"I know. But I do think she wants this. She's just kept it to herself a lot because she didn't think I did."

"Are you going to tell her?" Avery asked.

"I tell her everything." Kenzie stood. "She's my wife. Sometimes, it takes me a minute, or I run things by someone else first, but I always tell her everything. That's just the way we've always been with each other ever since she helped me carry my luggage at Peyton's adult summer camp all those years ago." Kenzie's smile was wistful now. "I want to have her baby, guys."

"Then, go get busy," Maddox said, standing up. "Well, you know what I mean."

"Thanks, Mad. I'm sorry I interrupted. Lennox was sleeping, and I just thought I needed to get some advice. I want to talk to her about it tonight. She's normally the romantic one, but I'm going to pick up some new candles and pull out all the stops because this is a really big deal."

"It is, and I can't wait to meet my future godson or goddaughter?" Maddox said in the form of a question.

"Nice try." Kenzie chuckled. "I'll have to talk to my wife about that first."

"Understood," Maddox said.

She approached Kenzie and gave her a long hug. She then must have whispered something encouragingly into Kenzie's ear because the woman hugged Maddox tighter and smiled. When they pulled away, Kenzie approached Avery and held out her hand for Avery to shake. Avery did and then smiled at her, knowing that Kenzie probably needed a little space when it came to strangers right now. The doorbell rang.

"Food's here," Maddox announced.

"Good. She's hungry for food and you, so get to the food now, Mad, so you can get to everything else later."

"Did you just make a joke, Kenzie?" Maddox asked.

"I did. I'm getting good at it," Kenzie said. Then, she opened the door. "That's for them." She hooked her thumb behind herself at Maddox and Avery. "Thanks, guys."

"Anytime, Kenz."

Kenzie walked past the delivery guy. Maddox took the food from the confused-looking man and closed the door behind him. Then, she turned back around to face Avery.

"Sorry, I had no idea she was planning on stopping by."

"It's okay. I just got off the phone with Tony and wanted to come look for you."

"Because you missed me?" Maddox teased as she placed the bag on the coffee table.

Avery thought for a moment before she moved to Maddox and wrapped her arms around her neck.

"Actually, yes. I don't even care if that makes me sound lame."

"It doesn't," Maddox told her. "Now, let's eat lunch. Then, we can take care of that other thing you're apparently hungry for." She lifted a sexy eyebrow at her, and Avery gulped.

CHAPTER 25

It WAS hours later when Maddox finally said a temporary goodbye to Avery. She knew it would only be a couple more hours until she would see her again, but she already missed her. Maybe it was stupid to have their first official date when neither of them had slept the night before, and Maddox had already been running on fumes, but she couldn't wait, and it appeared that Avery couldn't wait, either. Maddox crashed into her bed the moment she closed the door after kissing Avery goodbye. She set her alarm for two hours later, fell asleep instantly, and woke up to the annoying sound what felt like five minutes after her head hit the pillow. She had one second where she thought about going back to sleep because she desperately needed it, but that was quickly overtaken by the thought of seeing Avery again.

She got up and dressed in a pair of dark jeans and a light-gray sweater. It was dressy without being too dressy. She put on a pair of black flats with gray toes and grabbed her camera bag that operated as her purse when Maddox needed to bring some overnight stuff. She wasn't sure if she'd be staying over at Avery's, but she wanted to be prepared in case she received the invite. She had tucked her toothbrush, hairbrush, a pair of underwear, and a shirt into the smaller pocket of the bag, figuring she could borrow everything else from Avery.

"Oh," Maddox said when Avery opened the front door of her apartment.

They had agreed that Maddox would pick Avery up to give Avery more time to plan their evening since the woman had insisted on handling the details of their first date. Avery stood in front of her now, though, wearing a much fancier dress than the one she had worn the night before. It had black sequins on it and was strapless. Avery had on a pair of what looked to be two to three-inch black heels. Her dark hair was pulled back into a well-made braid that had been swirled into a bun and sprayed down into place, and her makeup was different than it had been the previous night, when it had hardly been there at all.

"Oh?" Avery asked. "Do I have something in my teeth?"

"No, it's just…" Maddox didn't know what to say.

It wasn't that Avery wasn't beautiful. Avery could never not be beautiful in her estimation. It was just that she didn't need the smoky eyes or the obvious fake eyelashes or heavy mascara. She didn't need the deep red lipstick or the fancy dress or shoes that were likely hurting her feet.

"I didn't expect you to get so dressed up," Maddox finally added.

"Tony helped me get ready," Avery said, motioning for Maddox to enter her apartment.

"Should I have gotten dressed up more?"

"No, you look perfect," Avery told her with a smile that told Maddox that this woman wasn't completely comfortable in her own skin right now. "So, this is my place. I can give you the tour, but it's really just an apartment, and we should probably get going. We have a reservation at Oceanic in twenty minutes. We don't want to be late."

"Oceanic?" Maddox questioned.

"Yeah, Tony has a friend that works there. I didn't ask what kind of friend, exactly, but he was able to get us a reservation."

"That's a pretty nice place," Maddox said, downplaying it.

Oceanic was one of the five-star restaurants this city

was known for. Maddox had been there once before with Peyton and Dani, and it had cost an arm and two legs. It had also been pretentious and not one of Maddox's favorite places.

"And there's not a lot open because of the holiday today, but there's this—"

"Hey, Avery?" Maddox interrupted her, taking her hand.

"Yeah?"

"Can you tell me what's going on right now?"

"What do you mean? I'm just grabbing my purse, and we can go."

"Babe, I thought we were just going to have a chill date. What's going on? Do you really want to go to Oceanic? If you do, I'm there, I promise. It just doesn't seem like you."

"It's not, but I thought it might be you," Avery told her.

Maddox squinted at her and said, "Really? Why?"

Avery leaned against the wall behind her and said, "I don't know. I think Tony got in my head a little."

"What did he say?" Maddox placed her hands on Avery's hips.

"That you're a world-renowned photographer who is best friends with pop stars, models, and actresses, and has dated supermodels."

"Oh, babe," Maddox began with a smile. "Your brother is an idiot."

"I know that, but what makes you say it?" Avery asked.

"Did you get all dressed up like this because he got in your head?"

"Maybe? Do I look that hideous?"

"Avery, you could never look hideous to me. You're beautiful. I just don't need all the trappings. I loved how you looked staring out at the water, remember? You hardly had any makeup on. Your dress was all flowing, beautiful. To be clear, I also loved you this morning in a T-shirt and a pair of my boxers with no makeup on and wet hair. If you want to wear this and be fancy, that's fine with me, but I like you when you look like you; not how your brother thinks I'd want you to look." Maddox leaned in and pressed her lips to Avery's cheek. "You're perfect to me just the way you are."

"Really?" Avery asked softly.

"Yes, babe. We still have a lot of getting to know each other to do, but I think you'll find out about me that I love a woman who just is who she is and doesn't give a crap what other people think."

"That's normally me. I've just never been with someone like you."

"What does that mean? Someone who's so crazy about you, she couldn't wait until she had a good night's sleep to see you again?"

"I guess," Avery said with a sweet laugh.

"Avery, do you want to go to Oceanic tonight?"

"Not really." The woman looked apologetic now. "I'd much rather sit on my sofa watching a movie while we cuddle up and maybe just order a pizza."

"That sounds like the best way to spend our first date."

"Are you sure?" Avery asked.

"Let's do this." Maddox pulled Avery away from the wall and turned her around. She kissed Avery's neck as she slid the zipper down on Avery's dress. "You change out of this dress, and if you want, hop in the shower to clean your hair and face. If not, that's fine, too." She kissed Avery again. "I'll order us some food and change into the clothes I brought with me. You change into something crazy comfortable, and we'll start a movie." Maddox kissed her again and turned Avery back around to face her. "I'll let you be the big spoon."

"Yeah?" Avery asked.

"And we'll pick a movie we've both seen already so that we can keep talking. I'll make sure you understand how little I care about makeup and fancy dresses, and you can tell me more about anything you want."

"That does sound like the best first date." Avery wrapped her arms around Maddox's neck. "Let me call the restaurant and cancel the reservation."

"Don't they charge for that?"

"Yes, but it's—"

"Make sure to tell them to put it on Tony's credit card then," Maddox said, kissing her forehead. "Go change. I'll be here when you get back."

"Hey, Mad?" Avery asked.

"Yeah?"

"Thank you."

Maddox winked at her and watched Avery disappear into what must have been her bedroom. Maddox used her phone to find a pizza place and ordered something she hoped Avery would like. She also got options just in case. Then, she pulled out her camera bag and slipped her T-shirt on over her head after removing her bra. She'd save the extra undies for the following morning. Then, she pulled her camera out, too, and placed it on the coffee table. When Avery emerged from her room, her hair wasn't wet, but it had been brushed out and now fell in full waves around her head. Her face was clean of makeup, and she was wearing a pair of boy shorts in purple with blue dots and a purple tank top.

"You look gorgeous," Maddox told her after she caught her breath. "Want to sit down with me?"

"Yes. And I should have told you before that you look great."

Avery sat next to her while Maddox picked up her camera and turned it on. She then turned her body to face Avery.

"What are you doing?" Avery asked as she laughed in nervousness.

"Taking your picture."

"Mad, I'm in my underwear."

"It's not for anyone else." Maddox pressed her eye to

the viewfinder. "I just want to capture you in a way that might allow you to see you how I see you." She clicked and clicked. "I can't believe I waited over six hours to kiss you." Maddox clicked a few more shots.

"Excuse me. *I* kissed you."

"That's right. You did." Maddox took several more pictures of Avery blushing, Avery smiling, Avery trying to put her hand in front of the lens, and Avery laughing. "Thank you, by the way."

"For kissing you?"

"Yes. I had my own in-my-head moment when I saw you talking to Val." She took a few more shots and put the camera down on the table. "We can look at those tomorrow morning after I take even more."

"What? More?"

"Yes, more; right when you wake up. You're dating a photographer now, Avery. You should probably get used to having your picture taken all the time."

"I hadn't even thought of that." Avery laughed. Then, she stopped. "So, we're dating?"

Maddox lifted Avery's arm around her shoulders and settled against her.

"Yes, we're dating."

"And… are we dating other people?"

"I don't want to date anyone but you."

"Neither do I."

"Good. Then, be a good girlfriend and help me pick a movie out that we've both seen a million times."

Avery kissed the top of Maddox's head. When the pizza arrived, they ate a couple of slices and a breadstick or two but put the rest in the refrigerator for later. They didn't finish the movie. Once they'd cleaned up their dinner, they retired to Avery's bedroom, where they slid into bed. Avery showed Maddox how to use the app for the first time, and neither of them bothered to set an alarm. Avery wrapped her arms around Maddox from behind and pulled her back against her warm body.

"This is a perfect first date," Maddox said after she had closed her eyes.

"Happy twenty-nine-hour anniversary," Avery joked.

"Just remember what we're doing for our forty-eight-hour," Maddox said.

Avery kissed Maddox's shoulder, her neck, and her jaw before she replied, "Oh, I'll remember."

When Maddox woke up the following morning, she took in Avery's sleeping form for several minutes before she climbed out of bed and went into the living room to grab her camera. She moved around the bed and took several pictures of her sleeping girlfriend. Avery stirred, thanks to the shutter clicking. When she opened her eyes, she used her hand to push the camera away.

"Mad, come on. I'm not even awake yet," she said in a voice heavy with sleep.

Maddox placed the camera on the bedside table and crawled back into bed on top of Avery, who was lying on her stomach. She then leaned down so that her mouth was pressed to Avery's ear.

"You don't want to show me your toys now?"

"Okay. I'm up."

EPILOGUE

THEY HADN'T done anything special for their forty-eight-hour anniversary or their seventy-two-hour anniversary unless they counted having hours upon hours of amazing sex, which Maddox surely did, but she didn't think that sex was technically an anniversary gift for her girlfriend or for her. It was amazing, though. That thing Avery had done during their first time still gave Maddox goosebumps when she thought about it. Hell, it sometimes gave her material to get herself off to when they had to be apart because Maddox was on a shoot out of town.

"What are you thinking about?" Avery asked.

"Nothing. Why?" Maddox asked back.

"You just got that look in your eyes you sometimes get when—" Avery squinted at her. "You're thinking about sex, aren't you?"

"What? No," Maddox lied terribly.

"Yes, you are. I can always tell when you're thinking about sex."

"Then, why even ask?" Maddox replied.

"You cannot be thinking about sex, Mad. We're babysitting," Avery said.

"And the baby is in bed. We're actually just sitting right now," Maddox replied as she wiggled her eyebrows.

"They'll be home any minute," Avery said, but her body moved from its sitting position to lie down on the oversized sofa.

"That's why you're lying down right now? Do you

have a thing for being watched that I don't know about?" Maddox moved Avery's legs out of her way so she could slide on top of the woman. "Are you secretly hoping they walk in on us?"

"No," Avery said, wrapping her arms around Maddox's neck. "But I was also thinking about sex, so…"

"Oh, really?" Maddox leaned down and kissed Avery's lips.

Every time she did this, Maddox felt like she was coming home. Avery was the best part of her morning, noon, and night; and that was saying something because Maddox loved her life. She loved her friends, her family, her career, and her new little godson, Liam. She loved all the new little ones in her life, and she knew that one day, she and Avery would be talking about having a little one of their own. They weren't quite there yet, but one day.

They heard the key in the door before they heard the laughter coming from outside it. Maddox shot up and off Avery, who sat back up and straightened her shirt and pants unnecessarily. Maddox rested her elbow on the arm of the sofa and her head on her hand, putting as much space between them as possible.

"Hey, guys," Lennox said, dropping keys onto the kitchen island. "How is he?"

"Fine. He's sleeping. That's what babies do. They sleep," Maddox replied, trying to cover.

"How was your first night away?" Avery asked them.

"Good," Kenzie said, walking up right next to Lennox. "I'm just going to check on him."

"Okay." Lennox kissed her cheek. Kenzie waved at them and made her way up the stairs. "She's such a good mom," Lennox added.

"How much of your night was spent talking about him?" Maddox asked as Lennox flopped down between them on her sofa.

"Pretty much all of it, but that's fine. It's the first night out. We'll get another little break when my parents come next week. I still can't believe they actually care enough about having a grandchild. The moment I told them I was naming him after Will, it's like they changed personalities. They would have been here already, but Dad was directing, so they'll meet him at six weeks old instead."

"He won't remember anyway," Maddox told her friend.

"I know, but they will. I want them to be involved in his life. Kenzie doesn't have any family. I want him to have grandparents."

"He will, Len."

"He's sleeping," Kenzie said as she came back down the stairs.

"He is an infant, babe. They do that a lot," Lennox said.

"Were we gone too long?" Kenzie asked, sitting down in the chair next to their sofa.

"You were gone for like two hours," Avery said and laughed. "We barely had time to finish the movie we were watching, and he's been sleeping the whole time."

"So, we expect to be paid in full, obviously," Maddox teased.

"Or, you should be grateful. We were watching Sienna and Jordan the other night for Peyton and Dani, and let's just say, Sienna is well on her way to her terrible twos." Lennox patted Maddox's thigh.

"Well, we should get going," Maddox stood. "We'll see you guys tomorrow?"

"We'll be there," Lennox said.

"He's probably going to be waking up in a minute. I'll just go check on him and get ready to feed him," Kenzie said, standing. "See you guys tomorrow, and thanks for watching him." Kenzie disappeared up the stairs.

"God, she's so damn cute sometimes. I love that adorable creature," Lennox said. "And Liam is just a little version of her. He has her eyes and her nose, and I love him so much."

"You are so tired right now, aren't you?" Maddox laughed. "Go upstairs with your wife and watch her feed your son, Len. We'll see ourselves out."

"Her boobs are huge now," Lennox told her.

"Okay. She's delirious," Avery said, laughing.

"We don't really sleep a lot these days," Lennox said, standing. "And I wish I could say it was because we're having all the sex."

"Well, that'll come back." Maddox patted her on the back.

"The doctor did just give her the all-clear," Lennox said and seemed to realize at the same time. "Okay. I'll see you guys tomorrow. Bye." She moved quickly to the staircase.

"Unless you want to hear their sex sounds, we should probably be going now," Maddox told Avery.

Avery just laughed, and they walked hand in hand out of the house.

***

"Does it suck, or is it cool that our anniversary will always be on New Year's Eve?" Avery asked.

"A little of both, I guess. I think it just depends on what, if anything, we do each year."

"That's true. We could always celebrate it before or after," Avery told her.

"Next year, maybe we can go somewhere after Christmas, just you and me. We can have a whole week to celebrate," Maddox suggested. "If we think about it soon, I can make sure to take the time off and not pick up any jobs for January. We can have the whole month together."

Avery loved that Maddox was talking about their next anniversary already. One year with Maddox Delaney hadn't been enough. She wanted another and another with this woman.

"That sounds nice, but will Peyton get mad at us for

skipping out on her party?" Avery asked, holding on to Maddox's hand as Maddox rang the doorbell.

"I don't think so. We can make sure to attend something else to make–"

"Hey, come in. Sienna is throwing a temper tantrum, and Jordan just threw up all over Dani, so she's changing," Peyton said, holding a crying Sienna against her hip.

"Somehow, I think this might be their last party for a while," Maddox said to Avery.

"What?" Peyton asked. "I can't hear you over my screaming toddler," she added, looking at Sienna. "Baby, come on. You're making mama look bad," Peyton told her daughter.

"Want me to take her?" Maddox asked. "She loves her Aunt Maddox."

"That she does," Peyton said and passed Sienna to Maddox, who held her against her hip.

Avery watched the young girl with the adorably curly blonde hair relax against Maddox's side.

"Show off." Peyton glared playfully at Maddox.

"Can I help with anything?" Avery asked as they walked into the house.

"I think this year is the opposite of last year. Instead of hundreds of people, it's going to be just the six of us and three kids. No caterers this time, but I made a bunch of food. And Kenzie and Dani aren't drinking, so I have cocktails and mocktails, too."

"I'm sure it'll be just as fun as last year," Avery said.

"Probably even more fun. I don't think I can handle another party like that," Peyton replied as they made their way into the living room. "What was I thinking?"

"I have no complaints," Maddox said. "I met this one because of that party."

Avery smiled over at her and asked, "Where are Lennox and Kenzie?"

It was so strange to her that she could now count these four women among her friends. Avery spent more time with them than she did with her own brothers and sister these days, acting as a babysitter with Maddox when they needed nights out, and she still hadn't quite gotten used to the fact that she was invited to their dinners, parties, and sometimes, just to hang out. A few afternoons, she had been invited even when Maddox had been out of town for work. These women were her friends now beyond her relationship with Maddox, and it was the first time in her life she had real female friendship.

"Hey, sorry. Jordan didn't care to just burp. He needed to vomit everything I'd just fed him back up," Dani said as she came down the stairs. "Happy New Year," she added.

"Mama," Sienna said when she saw Dani.

"Hey, baby." Dani reached out her arms and took her daughter from Maddox. "How would you like a snack before bedtime?"

Sienna didn't say anything. She just rested her face against Dani's neck.

"I'll take her," Peyton said. "You just dealt with baby vomit. I can take care of a tired baby yelling about having to go to sleep." She moved toward Dani, kissed the woman on the lips, and then took Sienna, who did look pretty tired. "And Len and Kenz are putting Liam down in Sienna's playroom."

"We just did," Lennox said, joining them in the room. "Kenzie just got a Happy New Year call from one of her friends from college, so she'll be down in a minute. Hey guys," Lennox said, reaching for Maddox and giving her a hug.

"Hi," Maddox greeted and hugged her back.

"Different than last year, huh?" Lennox asked Avery when she hugged her next. "I have a feeling we'll all be in bed by nine this time," she added.

"Well, you two might not." Dani sat on the sofa. "You don't have little ones keeping you up every night."

"No, we just have sex doing that," Maddox teased.

"Maddox!" Avery slapped her shoulder playfully.

"So, I'm going to ignore that," Dani said. "It'll be a pretty low-key night. The kids will be down soon, and we can just hang out before I pass out on this sofa. Then, Peyton will wake me up, and we'll go to sleep for a couple of hours before Jordan needs to feed, or Sienna wakes up crying because Jordan is crying. It's our new nightly ritual."

"And you love it," Maddox said with a smile.

"I do. It's exhausting and rewarding at the same time, and I love it. I also love that Len and Kenz had a little one. Liam and Jordan are going to be best friends."

"As soon as they can sit up on their own," Lennox said.

"And I'm thinking a June wedding for Sienna and Liam." Dani winked at Lennox.

"Well, he *did* tell me the other day that he has a thing for older women."

"Who does?" Kenzie asked as she joined them.

"You do," Lennox said. "You *did* marry me." Lennox pulled Kenzie down into her lap.

"I'm into an older *woman*; not older *women*. There's a difference," Kenzie said and kissed her on the lips.

"At least this party is starting after the sunset," Dani said, looking toward the window. "Last year, it felt like it went on for days."

"Do you want to go for a walk on the beach?" Maddox asked Avery, taking her hand.

"Sure," Avery replied.

"We'll be back in a bit. Don't have too much fun without us," Maddox told them.

They made their way out the back door, down the patio steps, and kicked their shoes off before their feet met the sand. It was a little cooler than it had been last year, but it was still Los Angeles in winter, so a sweater and jeans were just perfect. Avery pressed the side of her body against Maddox's as they walked toward the sand and then along it without saying anything for a while.

"Hey, can I ask you something?" Maddox asked as

they approached the rocks.

"Of course."

Maddox stopped walking and took both of Avery's hands in her own.

"So, we've been together for a year now."

"That's true," Avery replied, wondering why Maddox had gotten nervous all of a sudden.

"Babe, do you want to move in with me? We can find a new place. I don't mean you have to move into my place. I was actually thinking it would be better to find a place together; that way you can have a real office if you want, and I can maybe still have mine. I'd be cool with sharing one if you are, but I know you like your space when you're apping," Maddox rambled out.

She had taken to calling Avery's work *apping*, which was not a real word, and Avery loved that her girlfriend had made it up just for her.

"You want us to move in together?"

"I do. I was going to wait until midnight, kiss you first, and then ask, to make the whole thing special, but – I don't know – walking along this beach like we did last year has me all sentimental." Maddox paused and met Avery's eyes with her own. "I've already been looking for places."

"You have?"

"When I was in Paris for Fashion Week, I started looking stuff up. I have an idea of what we could afford."

"I'm not worried about the rent, Mad. We'd be fine there."

"I'm not talking about rent, babe." Maddox let go of one of her hands and cupped Avery's cheek. "I'm talking about a down payment."

"Down payment?" Avery checked. "You're talking about a house, Mad?"

"Yeah. Is that crazy?" she asked, still a little nervous.

"No, it's not crazy. I just wasn't expecting it. I thought we'd get an apartment together first. I mean, I'm at your place whenever you're in LA, anyway. I just thought I'd move in there and give up my place."

"You can. You can totally do that. I just feel like this is what I want, Ave." Maddox sounded so excited. "We've been together for a year. I know that's not all that long in the grand scheme of things, but I know what I want. I know I want us together, and I want that forever."

"Mad…" Avery said softly.

"I'm not proposing," Maddox explained. "I might, one day. I don't know; maybe you'll be the one to do that. I know how much you like to be the big spoon."

"You like it when I'm the big spoon," Avery teased her, taking Maddox's hips into her hands and pulling Maddox to her.

"I do like it. I like everything about you. I was looking at houses, and I just got really excited about the idea of us buying one together and making it our home."

"Well, we can afford it now that the app is live and working, and you're super famous and talented." Avery pressed her forehead to Maddox's.

"Move in with me, Avery. Make a home with me. Who knows? Maybe one day, we'll have a playroom for a little one of our own or at least a room for our little nieces and nephews to play in."

Avery kissed her briefly and said, "Okay."

"Okay?" Maddox pulled back to look at her.

"Yes, Mad. I want to move in with you."

"But, I mean about the whole thing. Do you want to just move in, or do you want to pick a new apartment, or do—"

"Let's look at houses together, Mad." Avery smiled at her, pulling Maddox back in for another kiss.

Maddox's hair was down, which meant Avery could run her hands through it before she lowered them to Maddox's back and slid them up and down as their tongues met.

"I have a few links I can send you," Maddox said when they pulled apart.

"Let's look at them when we get back to your place," Avery said.

"That sounds like a great way to start the new year." Maddox kissed her again.

Avery turned to look at the rocks off to the side and said, "I can think of another great way to start the new year."

"Seriously?" Maddox asked with a lifted eyebrow after she followed Avery's eyeline.

"There's not a raging party going on, and it's dark enough. Everyone else has done it, haven't they?"

"You planned this, didn't you?" Maddox asked as she took Avery's hand and began pulling her toward the rocks.

"And I can tell you're *so* against the idea," Avery teased as she laughed and followed Maddox, knowing she would follow this woman anywhere.

Over the past year, they'd fallen in love, fought over silly things and some serious things, too, met the families, talked about the future, and spent time abroad together for Maddox's job. Maddox had been by her side, helping her prep for one investor's meeting after another. Maddox was there to celebrate when Avery had gotten her Series A funding, when she had hired her first employee, and when the app officially hit the app store. Maddox had also been there the first time the app went down and Avery went through the roof because the second developer she had hired screwed up her code. Avery had yelled at Maddox, taking it out on her for no reason. Later that night, they'd made love after Avery had apologized to her. It was also the first time she had said the three words she'd been dying to say to Maddox, and it was the first time Maddox said them back.

Avery had been there when Maddox was so exhausted from traveling from London to Paris to Toronto to Egypt, that the woman had dark circles around her eyes and wasn't eating or sleeping well. She had helped Maddox sleep by lying close to her, wrapping her arms around her, and whispering softly into her ear. She'd fed her home-cooked meals, and she had been the one to tell her, even though all of Maddox's friends also thought she needed to stop, that it was time for a break from fashion photography. Maddox had then taken a two-month vacation from the world of fashion and had focused on her passion: nature. Well, nature *and* Avery.

Avery had a camera in her face almost daily. Maddox had three of her favorite shots of Avery in her apartment. Dani had even taken one of them together after Maddox had instructed her on the exact technique she had wanted, and it hung on Maddox's wall and was on a table in Avery's apartment. As Maddox pressed Avery gently against a very tall rock, Avery thought about how they would have two copies of that photo in their place now.

Maddox pressed her body into Avery's. Her lips were on Avery's neck. It was one of Maddox's favorite spots to kiss, and Avery loved it. She also loved when Maddox's tongue came out and licked to her earlobe before sucking it into her mouth. Avery moaned as she reached for the belt on Maddox's jeans. She unbuckled it and then unbuttoned and unzipped the jeans within seconds. Maddox chuckled against Avery's skin at her eagerness. Then, Maddox undid Avery's belt, button, and zipper, and pressed her own thigh between hers.

"I know we just did this last night, but I'm going crazy right now," Maddox said. "Maybe it's being here, where we met, on the anniversary of the night we met, but I want you."

"You have me. I'm here." Avery slid her hands into Maddox's pants but over her underwear and cupped her ass, pressing Maddox more into her.

"I want you."

"I know, babe. I—"

"No, I want to taste you," Maddox told her.

"Oh," Avery said, offering a wicked smile. "Here?"

"Yes, here."

Maddox slid Avery's jeans down her hips. Then, Avery

kicked them off of her ankles, and Maddox lowered her underwear, lifting Avery's leg to do the same with the pink bikinis. Maddox kept the leg lifted and placed it on her shoulder before she pressed her mouth to Avery's center and breathed her in.

"God," Avery let out in a husk. "I thought maybe you'd touch me against the rocks, and I'd like that, but I didn't expect you to go down on me like this."

"Are you complaining?" Maddox asked before she slid her tongue up and down.

"No, this is what I really wanted. I love when you do this to me."

"You love when you can press my face to your clit and tell me to lick it," Maddox said. "It's okay, Ave. You can do it."

"Lick it," Avery told her.

"Yes, ma'am," Maddox replied and did as she was told.

Avery held Maddox's head against her sex, encouraging the woman closer, telling her to lick, suck, and flick until she felt her orgasm begin to build. She loved this part of their sex life. She loved that Maddox allowed her to take control sometimes and, somehow, always knew when Avery needed her to take control. When she came, it was hard, and she was holding Maddox's head tightly against her. Maddox helped with her panties and her jeans, bringing them up with her as she stood. Then, Maddox kissed her mouth hard, and Avery tasted herself on her lips.

She turned them around until Maddox was against the rock. Then, she slid her hand inside and stroked Maddox. She knew her girlfriend loved watching her hand moving beneath her jeans, and Maddox's eyes lowered instantly to watch Avery work. She gasped and moaned as Avery slid around in her wetness before she stroked her clit more fully and with intent. Maddox came quickly, tugging Avery closer and kissing her through her orgasm. Then, Avery slid her hand out of Maddox's jeans and placed it under her shirt on her skin so as not to get Maddox's wetness on her shirt.

"I love you, Mad."

"I love you," Maddox said, kissing her again.

"We should get back inside," she breathed out.

"Probably," Maddox said, kissing her once more. "You need to wash your hand."

"You need to wash your face," Avery replied.

Maddox helped get the sand off of Avery's jeans. Avery licked her fingers clean, which she knew turned Maddox on.

"You're being really mean right now." Maddox laughed at her as they left the rocks.

"I'll be happy to do whatever you want later," Avery told her.

They made their way back into the house, holding hands. When they got to the living room, all four women were sitting there and looked up at them.

"Well, how was it?" Peyton asked.

"The walk was nice," Maddox told them.

"Yeah? How was the sex?" Lennox asked.

"What? We didn't–" Avery tried.

"You've got four moms who pretty constantly run upstairs to check on their kids and happen upon the open doors of the balcony pretty often. You want to rethink that lie?" Dani asked with a supermodel-eyebrow lifted at them accusingly.

"Fine. It was hot," Maddox said. "And we'll probably do it again later."

"Maddox!" Avery yelled and laughed.

***

Several hours later, when all the women were exhausted and probably should have gone to bed, they were huddled around the TV in the living room, watching the ball about to drop, when Maddox got an idea.

"Hey, Ave?"

"Yeah?" Avery asked her.

"Want to jump in the ocean with me?" She smiled at her girlfriend.

"Now?" Avery asked.

"Mad, are you serious?" Peyton asked.

"Shit. It's Jessica," Lennox said, pointing at the TV.

"Oh, yeah. Her first movie is coming out soon," Maddox told them. "She's probably doing promo work for it."

"How do you know that?" Dani asked.

"We're not on the best of terms, but we email every now and then. She told me about it in one of them." Maddox turned her attention back to Avery. "So, ocean?"

"Again?"

"It can be a tradition." Maddox shrugged.

"We've only got about thirty seconds to decide," Lennox said.

"Let's do it," Peyton said and stood. "Come on, babe. Let's do one crazy thing tonight."

"It's so cold, Pey. Remember how cold it was last year?" Dani said but stood, too.

"I remember how I kept you warm after," Peyton replied, pulling Dani into her. "And I'll do it again. I'll always keep you warm, baby." She kissed her wife.

"And you?" Lennox asked Kenzie. "You led the charge last year. Are you interested in this insanity?"

"That depends." Kenzie stood.

"On what?"

"Will you keep me warm, too?"

Lennox stood, pulled Kenzie into her, and said, "Always, Kenz." She then kissed her briefly.

"What do you say, Avery?" Maddox asked her.

"Only if you keep me warm, too." Avery stood up.

"That's your job." Maddox pulled her girlfriend into her body. "You're the big spoon, remember?"

All six women made their way outside, kicking off their shoes as they went. They lined up at the shore with Peyton keeping an eye on the countdown on her phone. They counted down when it got to ten, and at the stroke of midnight, Peyton dropped the phone in the sand, they took their partners' hand, and they ran into the water, starting the new year with a new tradition. When Maddox came up out of the waves, still holding on to Avery's hand, she turned to her and pulled Avery against her own body.

"Happy New Year. I love you, babe."

"I love you, Mad."

Made in United States
Orlando, FL
14 November 2021